THE HOMEC

Recent Titles by Grace Thompson

The Pendragon Island Series

CORNER OF A SMALL TOWN*
THE WESTON WOMEN*

The Valley Saga

A WELCOME IN THE VALLEY
VALLEY AFFAIRS
THE CHANGING VALLEY
VALLEY IN BLOOM*

DAISIE'S ARK*
FAMILY PRIDE*
SEARCH FOR A SHADOW*
SUMMER OF SECRETS*

* available from Severn House

THE
HOMECOMING

Grace Thompson

This first world edition published in Great Britain 1997 by
SEVERN HOUSE PUBLISHERS LTD of
9–15 High Street, Sutton, Surrey SM1 1DF.
First published in the USA 1997 by
SEVERN HOUSE PUBLISHERS INC., of
595 Madison Avenue, New York, NY 10022.

British Library Cataloguing in Publication Data
Thompson, Grace
  The homecoming
  1.Romantic suspense novels
  I. Title
  823.9'14 [F]

  ISBN 0-7278-5189-6

Typeset by Hewer Text Composition Services, Edinburgh.
Printed and bound in Great Britain by
Hartnolls Ltd, Bodmin, Cornwall.

Chapter One

From the gate of her Aunt Stella's cottage, Lydia looked up at the ruined castle, impressively large from where she stood. It had been there, looking out over the sweep of the bay for more than seven centuries and looked solid enough to last another seven. Behind her she could hear her mother and aunt arguing. Auntie Stella pleading, her mother tearful and determined.

"But Annie," Stella said patiently. "I have to do my shopping. And I always meet my friends for a chat on a Wednesday, you know this so why are you so difficult? And what about your Lydia? This is her half day and she's got things to do. Working all the hours she does, you should consider her time if not mine!"

"I don't feel well enough to travel home without Billy. I'll wait here until Billy comes and fetches me."

"You'll have to sit on your own then. I'm off to the shops. Lydia, if she has any sense, will go home without you!"

Annie Jones smiled. She knew Lydia wouldn't leave her alone.

Lydia's mother was what many secretly called a 'willing invalid'. There wasn't an apparent reason why she was unable to walk far, or why she had to spend so much of the year in bed, but since

Lydia, her only child, was born, she had been 'indisposed'.

Lydia listened to the exchange and sighed, her deep blue eyes lacking their usual cheerfulness, her long, light brown hair screening her dismay from her aunt. Dad would be disappointed not to see her when he got home from work. He'd have to change – because Mam didn't like him to come in his working clothes – and come to fetch her, when he had hoped to go straight to the allotment for an hour or two. It seemed that even her father's brief Wednesday respites were to be lost.

All winter, Annie stayed in her bed, with her sister, Stella calling in each day to check all was well and spending most of the day with her. During the all too brief summer, she was taken by taxi from her home overlooking the bay, to the home of her sister Stella, to stay there until Billy went by taxi to collect her. Auntie Stella, Lydia thought, was a saint!

Without the assistance of that patient lady, Lydia would have been unable to work. She had stayed at home looking after her mother since leaving school until one day, when she had reached the age of eighteen, her father had insisted they found a different way of dealing with their problem. Stella willingly agreed to help them and during the winter months taxied to their home and stayed with Annie until Billy returned from work.

Every day during the summer, apart from week-ends, Annie was taken by taxi to Stella to stay until Billy arrived by taxi to take her home again. She refused to go with anyone but Billy except on Wednesdays, when she allowed her daughter to escort her. Now Wednesdays were no longer a break in routine, for either Stella or Billy.

Because it was easier for Stella, the summer regime continued as long as they could persuade Annie it was still summer. It was already October and they all knew that it wouldn't be many more weeks before Annie refused to leave her bed, and Stella would have the extra work involved in coming to stay with her.

"At least I can get on with my own work while she stays with me," she had confided to Lydia. "Having to come to you means so much of my time spent out of the house."

"Luckily it's a mild Autumn, we should manage for a while longer."

Lydia sighed as she watched her aunt set off to do her shopping. They both knew that the stubborness of Wednesday was the beginning of the end of their summer arrangement and any day now, Annie would settle herself into her winter hibernation.

"Lydia, can you fetch a drink? A glass of water will do if you haven't time to make a cup of tea," Annie called. Lydia made the tea and returned to stare out over the road to the castle. She didn't often become irritable with her mother but today she had planned to do so much. With Glyn coming home soon, she wanted to catch up with her work so she was free to be with him. Or as free as her mother's 'illness' would allow.

Glyn Howe was the brother of Tomos who, with his father Gimlet Howe ran the local taxi service. Her family and theirs had always been close. Her father, Billy Jones, had been friends with Gimlet Howe since they were children and all her life, Gimlet's sons, Tomos, who ran the taxi service, and Glyn, who was in the navy, had been an important part of her life. The romance between herself and Glyn had evolved out of a contented childhood in which the brothers were her protectors. She loved the Howes dearly but Glyn was the dearest of all and tomorrow he would be coming home to marry her. She was irritated at the change in her plans for the afternoon. She had intended washing her hair and generally preparing for his return.

From her pocket she took Glyn's most recent letter. Received more than a month ago, it had been read and re-read so often she could have recited the four pages without unfolding them, but she read it again, trying to see if there was something she had missed, some reason for his failing to write. His words were less loving and there was none of the usual talk about their future.

Lydia was a small, slim twenty-two-year-old with masses of light brown curling hair and large blue eyes which showed latent humour, and the innocence of youth. She had no experience of flirting and no long list of boyfriends. For as long as she could remember she had loved Glyn Howe.

She heard voices and walked to the middle of the road to look up at the castle gate. A group of workmen were walking along the top of the high wall, looking through the battlements, pointing, discussing something which she guessed were repairs. The local paper had reported that the place was to be closed for several months while the structure was reinforced and railings added. Fears had been expressed over the safety to the public and work was due to begin the following Easter.

The men came down towards the gate near her aunt's house as a council lorry arrived and one of the men removed a roll of wire netting. As she watched, they fixed the wire netting over the top of the gate which they then locked with a pair of padlocks, before climbing onto the back of the lorry and being driven off. When Stella returned from her brief shopping trip, Lydia told her what had happened.

"So, the castle ground is no longer a place for people to kiss and cuddle, walk their dogs or to sit and eat lunch."

"Nor a place where children can play," Lydia said.

"Oh, you're wrong about that, love. Look up by there." Stella pointed to the towering outer wall of the castle below which were allotments. Walking along the narrow path outside the castle and a little above the neat allotments, pressing themselves against the walls was a group of children armed with home-made bows and arrows, and long, pointed sticks. "Neville Nolan and his gang for sure," Stella laughed. "Take more than a few workmen and a couple of padlocks to keep that lot out!"

"Is there any chance of us going home d'you think?" Lydia asked.

Stella shook her greying head. "I tried again to persuade her but she's insisting on waiting for your dad. Billy hoped to spend a couple of hours on the allotments didn't he? Fat chance he'll have by the time she's home and sorted. I'm just off to see my friend for an hour, you'll be all right, love? Promised her I did."

"Mr Howe is working there already. Clearing a plot for planting his broad beans no doubt. I'd better go and tell him Dad won't be coming. Mam won't miss me for a minute or two."

Stella slipped on her coat again and chuckled. "I wouldn't bet on that, love."

Gilbert Howe, or Gimlet, as he was usually called, had an allotment next to Billy's and they were friendly

5

rivals for the first and best produce. It was exciting to think of Gimlet Howe being her father-in-law in a few months time. Glyn, who was his youngest son, was leaving the navy for good and the young couple planned to marry within the year.

Lydia walked up the lane to the smaller gate which opened onto the allotments, and walked towards Gimlet, who was shouting at the group of boys led by Neville Nolan.

"Clear off the lot of you! I won't tell you again, mind!" he was shouting. Jeering, blowing raspberries and making thumb-to-nose gestures the boys of Neville's gang were defying him.

"Over the fence they came, traipsing right across your dad's allotment and kicking at his winter cabbage. They walk through the place as if they own it and them just been told to stay away from the castle by the men from the council," Gimlet said angrily. "Fat lot of good putting locks on the gates, it's them boys they ought to padlock, mind!"

"I don't think Dad will have time to join you today, Mr Howe," Lydia said. "Mam's playing up again. Won't go home with me, insists on waiting for Dad."

"Poor old Billy. His weeds will be hiding those leeks completely if he doesn't get here soon." He handed her a hoe. "Come on, girl, there's no point in you standing around too. That chickweed is growing as we watch! If she shouts for you she can't be heard from here."

Lydia tied back her long hair with a scarf and for a while they worked together, exchanging the latest news of Glyn, who was most lax with his letter-writing of late.

"Coming home soon he is," Gimlet explained, "so

6

there's less need to write when he'll be able to tell us himself."

"I can't wait," Lydia smiled. "This is the longest he's been away. Seven months is a long time."

"The longest and the last, love. A few weeks and he'll be settled in his job with Howe's taxis and home every day so you're sick of his ugly face."

"Never. I'll never be anything but glad he's back home."

It was six o'clock before Lydia, Billy and Annie were back home and almost eight before Annie was settled for the evening. They ate a scratch meal, as Lydia hadn't been home in time to prepare properly and at nine, Billy said, "Will you be all right if I slip out for a pint with Gimlet?"

"Go quiet so Mam doesn't hear or she'll be on all the time you're out," she said. She smiled as he tip-toed down the stairs to the kitchen and down the steps to the seafront. From the bay window she waved as he hurried to The Pirate to join Gimlet Howe and their friends.

Woodland skirted the castle on two sides, broken in places by paths and opening out where the allotments had encroached. On the side that faced the sea, a tall man climbed up through the thickly overgrown trees and brambles. He moved slowly and with hardly a sound, following a path regularly used by walkers and children. The fencing was new, placed with the intention of keeping people out, but it was already sagging where people had climbed over, and he vaulted it with ease.

The tall, well-built man was almost invisible in the darkness. His face, half hidden by a raised collar, was camouflaged by shadows. His feet made hardly a sound. He walked without showing a light; his eyes catlike, observing the bumps and irregularities so he moved without stumbling. He skirted the castle field using the bushes and the low walls for cover.

On reaching the Chapel block he climbed up and moved close to the wall and worked his way right around the great stone building. Then he stopped and stared upwards, frowning. He had to get inside. If workmen were going to start disturbing the ground he had to get there first and move something that had lain there for years.

He wondered if he would remember the place. The trees had grown making the exterior of the castle look different, so perhaps the inside had changed too? Would he know the actual spot where he had buried his secret? He had to. If it was found by the workmen there would be an enquiry which would lead unerringly to him. A police investigation was something he could well do without.

The night was utterly dark, low clouds obliterating the sky and the dampness creating a fog which made hazy puffballs of the street lights. He moved down to the gate opposite Stella's cottage, abandoned an attempt to climb it because of the freshly fixed netting, and returned the way he had come. Something would have to be done to discourage those boys whom he had seen earlier. Something effective and soon.

Lydia Jones loved the scene from the front window of the bay-fronted cottage high above the sea shore. She could see the whole of the great curved bay, looking over the houses and hotels along the seafront, the boats lying alongside the footpath and beyond, the sea and the steel town opposite. Further still the hills showed; range after range, into the distance where they finally disappeared into the blue haze. She knew she would never tire of it and that was one reason she wanted to live with her parents after she and Glyn married. The bedroom which would be theirs was above this room, with the same view.

The day was dying, the colours fading. Already, as she watched, the hills were slowly melding into each other and taking the colour of the evening mists. Lights around the pier were beginning to prick the scene, artificially bright in the approaching darkness. She felt no sadness at the departing light and the disappearance of the view. This would be the last day without Glyn. Tomorrow, he was coming home.

She saw her friend, Molly Powell, running past, back to the house she shared with Mr and Mrs Frank. Molly didn't hear her knocking on the window and Lydia smiled. Her friend had been off meeting her mysterious boyfriend no doubt. She wondered vaguely why Molly refused to tell her who he was. Molly Powell and she had been friends since their first day at school and had shared each other's most confidential secrets. This was the first time Molly had held a secret from her. Her mystery man must be very special.

Closing the curtains with regret, she turned away from the view and glanced at the old brass-bound box in the corner behind the piano. It had been her grandfather's sea-going chest now doing duty as her 'bottom drawer'. Inside was a collection of household linen; tablecloths, sheets, pillowcases and towels; all gathered ready for her wedding day. There was also a set of underwear, carefully wrapped in blue tissue. Pure silk and brought for her from Hong Kong by one of her father's sailor friends. She shivered with excitement at the prospect of wearing it for Glyn.

After running down to the kitchen to check that the cawl she was making for supper was simmering nicely on the stove, she glanced once more out of the window, pulling the curtains around her face and peering into the now artificially lit street. The lights made it possible to recognise the familiar figure of Tomos Howe, Glyn's brother who ran the taxi service, walking past. He would be on his way to collect his father, Gimlet, from The Pirate. Dad would be walking back with them. Time to set the table.

The smile faded from her face as a plaintive voice from upstairs called, "Your father not home yet, Lydia? Time he was home."

How did she always know when Dad was out? Lydia marvelled. Crept down the stairs like a breath of air he had. "Not yet, Mam. I saw Tomos going to fetch Mr Howe, so I expect Dad'll come now soon. Supper's ready," she added.

"I couldn't eat a thing. I feel so tired today, love. I didn't sleep last night. Will you fetch one of my tablets?"

"Mam, you can't have a tablet. The doctor says you can only have three and you'll want one at bedtime."

"I can't hear you, you'll have to come up. It wears me out, shouting down the stairs all the time."

"In a minute, Mam," Lydia shouted back. "I'm just stirring the cawl." Ignoring the request, Lydia went once more to look out of the window. Since coming home from work two hours ago she had been up to her mother seven times and every time it was unnecessary. Thank goodness Dad would soon be home. Mam would settle then.

She saw Gimlet Howe and her father approaching and besides them, Tomos. But, she realised with a great lurch of shock and delight, it wasn't Tomos, but Glyn! How could she not have recognised him before? He no longer wore naval uniform, of course, and in her mind's eye she still had him dressed as a sailor. How stupid of her not to know at once it was him. A day early and him not giving word, so he could surprise her.

She felt flustered now he was actually here and she rushed to touch up her lips and add a little colour to her cheeks, and there was time for a swift comb through her hair. She fluffed her curls out a little, stood on tiptoe to check briefly in the mirror over the fireplace, then ran down the stairs through the small kitchen on the ground floor. She realised she was holding her breath, listening to the group approaching. Feet ringing on the stone steps, men's voices, laughter, the door opening and he was there, smiling and looking so handsome she forgot to breathe again.

She wanted to run into his arms and feel his lips on her own, but her father was bustling them all in.

"Is there enough supper for a couple more, love?" Billy asked.

"Plenty, Dad. Welcome, Mr Howe." Then she saw that Tomos was with them. "Come in, Tomos, unless your wife is expecting you back?"

"Off visiting her mam, as usual," Tomos said, glancing at his father, exchanging disapproval.

Lydia hardly heard what was said, she was looking at Glyn, waiting for his smile that was hers alone, but he seemed to be ignoring her. He looked everywhere except at her eager face, going up the stairs to the living room and standing against the velvet curtains like a stranger.

"Try and persuade your Mam to come down, Lydia," Billy said. "We'll make it a party."

"I'll get some beer, shall I?" Glyn suggested. Lydia's spirits fell. Only now he was come and already he was making excuses to get out.

"What about I call for Molly, she'd be glad to come and join the party, eh?" Billy added.

"I'll go," Tomos said and within a minute of them arriving, feet clattered down the stairs, through the kitchen and out, boots ringing on the stone steps, their voices raised to reach Lydia as she stood by the window.

What was the matter? Why hadn't Glyn rushed and hugged her and smothered her with kisses? Surely the presence of the others hadn't stopped him? It never had before. She stood there, the excitement draining from her like a leaking balloon.

Determinedly concealing her disappointment, she went down to the kitchen and cut more bread. Four extra to feed, she forced her mind to deal with practicalities. Thank goodness she'd bought an extra loaf. There was a sponge cake, a tin of fruit, ice-cream, that would have to do.

She was still in the kitchen when the brothers returned with Molly. She was tense, waiting while Tomos and Molly went straight up to find a seat around the table. Now, at last she'd be alone with Glyn. She turned to look at him, her arms already raising to hug him, but he backed away. She failed to hold back a gasp of dismay as, without more than a half-smile, he followed them.

Carrying the extra plateful of bread, Lydia went

up, finding every step was agony, wondering how she would sit through this meal with Glyn treating her so distantly. Seven months was a long time to be parted, but it surely didn't explain this?

Annie was helped down the stairs and sat for a while, playing with her food before complaining of backache and returning to her bedroom. The awful evening continued, Lydia afraid to look at Glyn, knowing something was wrong, listening to Billy and Gimlet reminiscing and coaxing stories from the others, trying to join in the laughter.

She dealt with the food like an automaton, hardly aware of what was being said. Every time she went downstairs to the kitchen for further supplies she expected Glyn to offer to help, to follow her down, embrace her, kiss her, tell her how glad he was to be home. But she alone dealt with the meal, like a paid servant, she thought bitterly. The others seemed apart, enjoying the unexpected party and seemingly unaware of her distress.

Billy went to fetch a couple more flagons and it was after eleven before Molly, Gimlet, Tomos and Glyn all stood to leave. At the door, Glyn avoided her attempt to take his hand and only whispered, "Tomorrow we must talk," before following the others down the wide stone steps that would take them down to the seafront.

What had happened? Why had loving letters become ordinary and ceased altogether? What had changed in the seven months he was away? Had he found someone else? No, he would have been honest enough to tell her. She looked at her father dozing in the armchair. She knew that he had cheated on her mother, people talk in a small village and everyone knew Billy Jones had been with other women. And she and Glyn weren't even married, so there was less dishonour in him finding someone more attractive.

"Did you notice how quiet Glyn was, Dad?" Lydia asked when Billy was outing the fire before going to bed. "I have the feeling something is wrong."

"Never. Just a bit shy that's all. You and he haven't met for months and only letters to keep you in touch. It's natural he's a bit quiet, and with all of us here – damn me, girl, I didn't think! Bringing them all back here when you and Glyn wanted to be alone." He didn't tell her it was Gimlet and Glyn's persuading that had made him invite them. "What a thoughtless old fool I am!"

Lydia wanted to believe him.

"Billy?" Annie's wavering voice called. "When you coming up? You know I won't sleep till you do."

"Now in a minute, Annie," Billy called back patiently.

"Tell Lydia not to make a noise. I won't sleep a wink if she disturbs me when I'm off, mind."

When Billy had gone to bed, Lydia sat for a long time in the living room. She wondered if her father still found solace for his lack of a marriage in other women, and thought not. He was hardly out of her sight. He only went to The Pirate with Gimlet or sat with herself and Annie and, on occasions, Auntie Stella.

She crouched closer to the comforting warmth of the dying fire. She had dreamed about Glyn's homecoming for so long and now it had happened and had been nothing like she had imagined. They hadn't even kissed. After seven months apart it was such an anticlimax she wanted to cry. She was too wide awake to think of sleeping, so, careful not to disturb her mother, she made herself a cup of tea and sat, imagining tomorrow's meeting as a series of

14

wonderful, romantic moments. As dawn crept across the sea around the sides of the curtains and invaded the room, she slept.

Both Lydia and Molly worked on a market stall in the centre of town. Molly sold soaps and toilet requisites and Lydia sold knitted garments, some of which she made herself. All that following day, Lydia watched the kaleidoscopic crowds wandering through the varied stalls, expecting to see Glyn making his way towards her. At five o'clock he still hadn't come.

The last half hour dragged by and even when she left Molly keeping an eye on her stall to go and buy vegetables and meat for the evening meal, there was still a lot of time left to stand watching, waiting for Glyn. So many people asked her about Glyn, forcing her to invent reasons and excuses that she was more relieved than disappointed when it was at last time to fix the canvas around the stall and go home.

Getting the bus home was the usual crush and she and Molly had to stand, separated by several people. Speaking in hissing whispers as the bus trundled its way around the curve of the bay from town, out to the village nestling against the sea, they discussed Glyn's non-appearance. Molly suggested he was so upset about the lack of privacy the previous evening he was home, planning a surprise evening out.

"I hope you've got something quick to cook for supper," Molly grinned as they alighted at the bus stop below Lydia's house into the face of a rising wind. "You won't want to waste too much time cooking if Glyn's waiting, eh?"

But Glyn wasn't there and her father hadn't seen him either. Determined to speak to him, Lydia went to the Howes' terraced cottage facing the sea and with its back to the castle, but the house was deserted. Gimlet appeared later in the evening to walk to The Pirate with Billy but he shrugged when asked and insisted he knew nothing of Glyn's movements.

It was two more days before Glyn finally appeared, late one evening, when Lydia was settled listening to the radio and sewing up a newly completed cardigan.

The knock at the door was unexpected. Billy was already in bed. Prepared to see Molly, she gasped with surprise to see Glyn filling the doorway. He wasn't smiling and he made no attempt to kiss her, he just said, "Hello," and walked in through the kitchen and up the stairs to the living room. Flustered at his casual greeting, Lydia made a cup of tea in the downstairs kitchen before going up to join him. Putting down the tray she attempted a joke.

"So long since I saw you, do you still take sugar?"

"Lydia, I don't want to work on the taxis with Tomos and Dad."

"Oh, I thought you had arranged it all?"

"It can be un-arranged, can't it?"

She sat down, tense and frightened. Was he going to tell her he was not leaving the navy after all? That she would face months of separation, time and again in the years ahead? "Well, so what?" she said. "There are plenty of other things you can do."

"And I don't want to come here and live with your mam and dad," he added as if she hadn't spoken.

"Then we needn't. I'll have to live somewhere close, mind. Dad and Auntie Stella will still need my help with Mam after we're married."

"Lydia, there's no easy way to say this. I want to cancel our plans to marry next year."

16

"Well, there's no hurry. Give yourself time to settle into civvy street first, is it?"

"I mean cancel for good. I – I don't want to marry you."

"Glyn!"

"There's someone else, see. Cath is a girl I met six months ago and she and I – well. I know I can make her happy and – she needs me and . . . Sorry, I know I should have told you before this, but it isn't something I could put in a letter. I had to face you and try to explain."

"No need to explain anything. It isn't as if we're even officially engaged, is it? You and me, we've known each other since we were babies and—" Her attempt at being matter-of-fact failed. In a choking voice she added, "I think you'd better go now. We'll talk again but for now I—" she ran from the room, her hands over her ears shutting out his plea for her to listen to his explanations.

"Oh, Lydia, why do you have to make such a row?" Annie wailed. "Woken me up proper you have and what a night that'll mean." Lydia thought that her mother wouldn't be the only one to suffer a sleepless night.

Although it was late, she put on a coat and went back down stairs. Glyn had gone and she waited for a few moments to make sure he was out of sight then slipped out of the door, down the steps and onto the seafront.

The wind which had been gaining strength for days was rattling anything that was loose, prising weakened fabric from the older properties, beating a rhythm with a piece of broken shop blind and accompanying it with percussion from chinking metal and ropes slapping masts on the boats along the front.

There were few people about, as it was past midnight but she walked, staggering occasionally as an unexpectedly powerful gust hit her, and made her way to Auntie Stella's house. If, by any good fortune a light showed, she would knock and talk to her about Glyn's change of heart.

The house was in darkness. The bow window, which revealed its previous use as a shop, was black, not even a chink of light slipped through. She stood for a moment at the gate, wondering if her aunt was still awake and would respond to a gentle knock. She decided not and turned to look up at the castle. Such a pity it was closed. She forced her mind away from Glyn and considered trivialities.

The old castle was a popular place for people in the summer and even in winter, when there was a weak sun, they would come and sit to eat their lunchtime sandwiches, sheltered by its great walls. The children would miss it too. Ignoring warning notices and 'Keep Out' signs, they had climbed in via a window or by trusting the blanket of ivy, to play inside the shell; robots, aliens and other villains filling the air, the television heroes forming the basis for exciting games. She wished stupidly that she was a child again, free from the disappointments of growing up.

Now, as she stared up at the ancient building, her unhappiness created a less cheerful image. The ruin looked frightening, a storehouse of a thousand dark secrets, and she shivered. Trees were bending in the strong wind, groaning in their agony and their shadows danced behind street lights. It was a night when stories about ghosts haunting the place could be willingly believed.

She was hidden from view tucked in the shadow of

the gate and seeing the figures staggering down the slope leading down from the castle entrance made her press herself closer into the wall. Ghosts! They must be, her foolish mind insisted. These weren't shadows of trees. The figures were distinct and making their way purposefully to the gate across the narrow road from where she stood. Afraid to breathe, she watched with rising fear as the shadowlike figures became recognisable as two people. But they couldn't be real, flesh and blood people, some atavistic hysteria insisted.

Her feet refused to obey her when she felt the need to run, and she pressed more tightly against the ivy-covered garden wall. Then laughter rang out; a man's laughter. And someone said, "Hush you daft 'aporth, you'll wake the neighbours," and she knew the voice.

"Molly?" she called.

Perched on top of the castle gate, now without its recently placed wire-netting, one of the figures stopped. The other, close behind, turned and ran back up the slope towards the castle. "Molly?" Lydia called again.

"Hush, Lydia! Want to wake your Auntie Stella do you?"

"What are you doing in there? And at this time of night!"

"Don't be soft, girl. What d'you think we've been doing, making daisy chains?"

"That man," Lydia said as Molly came to join her, "your new boyfriend, is he?"

"Been following us, then?"

"Of course not! I couldn't sleep and came hoping to find Auntie Stella still up."

"Seen Glyn then, have you?" Molly asked with

sympathy in her voice. "Spoken to you about –
things? There's sorry I am, Lydia."

"He's told me we're finished but, how did you
know?"

"I-I saw, who was it now?" she frowned. "Oh, yes,
your dad and Gimlet were talking. They said Glyn
was coming to find you and tell you it's all over
between you. Sorry I am, but if he isn't sure, then
it's best for you to find out now rather than when
you are married. There's a mess that would be for
sure. Being married to someone you don't love is no
joke, believe me."

Lydia knew that Molly's parents had separated and,
after living with an aunt for a few years, Molly had
lived in a succession of rooms before settling down
with Mr and Mrs Frank.

"You walking home?" The two friends linked arms
against the still ferocious storm and walked down the
hill past silent shops to the seafront.

"Who is he?" Lydia asked, when she had exhausted
the subject of her disappointment. "Why are you
keeping him such a secret?"

"You won't let on if I say?"

"Tell me."

"Married he is and stuck with a wife he's never
loved. That's why you should be glad for Glyn being
honest and not getting you and himself into a mess
that's hard to escape from."

"I can't believe Glyn doesn't love me. We've been
together since we were children."

"Perhaps that's why. You've just drifted into
expectations of marriage. Believe me, Lydia, an
unhappy marriage is a terrible trap." A gust of
wind sent them staggering into a shop doorway
and laughing, Molly added, "Best to have some

20

fun like I do and avoid the ties that can strangle happiness."

"Is that where you meet? Up at the castle?"

"It was difficult for a while, with the gate being locked and the great stretch of wire over the top increasing the height. But since Neville Nolan stole the wire to mend his father's chicken coop, we've managed all right."

"Aren't you frightened?"

"That's part of the fun, creeping around the old walls, walking through the woods, imagining ghosts and clinging to each other in pretended fear. It's a damn sight more fun than being home watching telly and washing his socks!"

Lydia didn't dare admit that caring for Glyn with small tasks like washing his socks had been a part of her now shattered dream.

The days that followed Glyn's visit were difficult for Lydia. She had told so many people about his homecoming and the imminent engagement that it was a constant nightmare having to explain to everyone who remarked on the lack of a ring, that the romance had ended. Seeing Glyn when he walked past the house with his father caused stabs of pain which she thought would never ease.

Her father never mentioned it, being of the opinion that it was better to say too little than too much. Her mother thought differently. Every time she spoke to her daughter it was to tell her how fortunate she was, and how thankful she should feel to have escaped from a man who obviously did not deserve her. Annie tried to speak with sympathy for her daughter but in her heart she was relieved that the wedding was off.

When Lydia had been born, Annie had not been

prepared for the pain. The agony was so unexpected she had screamed and screamed and insisted she was dying. Then, when it was all over and she was told she could get out of bed, she had collapsed. It was quickly discovered that it was nothing more than temporary weakness after the birth, exacerbated perhaps by nervousness and fear, but Annie had been so shocked by the whole affair that she lacked confidence to stand on her feet except when Billy was there to support her. The fear had never left her and since then her life had been that of a semi-invalid.

Now she felt relief at the ending of Lydia's plans to marry. She knew that Billy wouldn't be able to cope alone and fear of what that might mean made it difficult to hide her joy at the worry being removed.

A few weeks after the ending of her wedding hopes, as October was ending in frosts and misty mornings and brief periods of glaringly bright sun, Lydia opened the door expecting to see Tomos come with his taxi to take her mother to Auntie Stella's and was startled to see Glyn standing there with that half smile which revealed his nervousness.

"What d'you want?" she asked casually. "Off to work I am, as soon as your brother comes for Mam."

"I'm taking her," he explained. "Tomos is off for the day." He stepped past her and went up to help Annie down. "It'll be me bringing her back tonight. About half five isn't it?" he said, not looking at her, but walking swiftly down the steps to the seafront.

Lydia was trembling from the unexpected encounter. "He couldn't even bear to look at me," she told

Molly when they were on the bus winding its way around the bay heading into town.

"More fool him! I bet this Cath of his is a real man-eater."

"She's welcome to him," Lydia lied. "I wouldn't have him back if he begged me!"

"Good on you. Have some fun like I do."

Glyn drove back to his parents' home after depositing Annie with Stella but he didn't go inside. He sat in the taxi and stared out across the houses and up onto the hill. He had to go away, and it was killing him. To leave this friendly place and start again among strangers, was a nightmare. He'd done all the travelling he wanted for a long time. Now, to have to find a new place and build a life, without Lydia, was something he didn't want to do, but there was no choice. He couldn't stay and see her every day without telling her he loved her and asking her to wait. He didn't need even to close his eyes to see the lovely face of Lydia, with her large gentle eyes full of reproach, wondering why he had stopped loving her and why he was going away.

Tomos appeared in the market soon after they opened.

"Glyn is giving me the day off as he probably told you," he explained. "Don't worry about your Mam, he won't forget to take your dad and fetch her."

"Where are you going?" she asked. "Have you and Melanie got something special planned then?"

"No, Melanie's off to Cardiff to see her Mam. I'm off to do a bit of fishing, get some fresh air."

"Lucky you," she smiled.

Molly closed her stall before lunchtime. She came

to explain to Lydia that she was feeling very sick and needed to go home before she collapsed. "A bilious attack, I suppose. I'll be all right if I can rest. Probably sleep the clock round."

Lydia promised to let the owner of the stall know and helped her friend to fix the canvas around the stall before watching her walk out of the market and head for the bus home. She was puzzled. Coming in that morning Molly had seemed perfectly well. But then, a bilious attack did come with very little warning.

Lydia went home alone, missing the lively chatter of her friend. She hurried from the bus to the house, rushing up the steps and into the house, then hesitated in the kitchen before calling to her parents that she was home. Tomos sometimes stayed and drank a cup of tea after bringing Annie back. All day she had been hoping Glyn wouldn't do the same. She couldn't face talking to him in her parents' presence as if nothing had happened. She dreaded meeting him, afraid of how she would react. Please, don't let him be here, she prayed silently. Then she was disappointed when he was not.

Chapter Two

Lydia and her father stood at the window of their living room and, looking out over the roofs of the houses and shops below, watched the group of ten-year-olds on the beach. They were pulling apart a wrecked rowing boat. They had begun by pelting stones at it, small ones at first then, as their determination intensified, the size of stones grew until they were staggering down over the rocks to the soft sand, and dropping their burdens onto the weakened craft. As boards loosened, the laughing boys used their hands and feet to tear its boards from the frame, red with effort and excited at the mess they were making.

Lydia could see anger clouding her father's expression.

"Hooligans the lot of them," Billy said. "Specially that Neville Nolan. They all want a good hiding, that's what!"

"Oh, Dad, they're only having fun."

"Fun you call it? Smashing something up? At their age I was working with my father, helping repair boats not smashing them! And sorting fish ready for market. The smell of that job put the girls off proper but I had to do it."

"It's really because it's Neville Nolan, isn't it?"

"Well, yes, I suppose it is. Little pest that he is. Nothing but cheek I get when I chase them out of

25

the allotments. Thank goodness the castle is closed and they can't get in there any more."

Lydia thought it wise not to tell her father that their access had been unaffected by the council's attempts to seal the place off.

Annie was home this morning as, being a Sunday, Lydia and Billy were not working. Her presence, constantly calling for attention, was the reason for her father's irritability. Several times each hour, Annie would call for something to be sent upstairs for her: 'I'm so dry, can I have a drink of water?' or 'I think I could manage a small biscuit,' or 'Can you help me to the lavvy? My legs have gone funny again.'

Lydia accepted that her mother would never be any different, but Billy still occasionally railed against the fate that had landed him with such a burden. It amazed her that he complained so rarely. Most of the time he seemed content. Sometimes she interrupted her father and her Auntie Stella talking quietly together and felt they had been discussing her mother. But that was a good thing. Billy needed to talk to someone and Annie's sister was the best person he could choose.

Lydia wanted to get on with lunch so she was free to spend a few hours with Molly, but seeing her father's unhappy mood, she stood silently beside him, a hand on his shoulder, talking to him. She looked small beside him, only five feet two and dainty, unlike Billy's heavily built five feet eleven. But she had her father's colouring, her light brown hair glinting with gold in the autumn sunshine streaming through the window. Her eyes did not have that far-seeing look of sailors and countrymen like his, but were as large and of the same deep blue. At that moment they showed more humour than Billy's sombre expression.

Lydia was hiding her own unhappiness from him.

Glyn's longed-for return when he finally left the navy had been far from the wonderful moment she had dreamed of. Most had believed it had been a mutual falling out of love, but for Lydia the grief was still fresh and causing an aching hurt, deep inside, hidden even from her closest friend. Molly pretended to understand but for her life was far simpler. Why couldn't she be as fancy-free as Molly?

Looking out of the window, sipping the strong tea she had made, they watched as the boys grew tired of their boat-wrecking and wandered off. A man was standing watching them and from the luggage he carried, he was newly arrived, or on the point of leaving.

"Who's that?" Billy asked, half closing his eyes against the glare.

"No one I know. Probably a tourist. Foreign by the look of him, with binoculars and a camera slung across his shoulders, and that rucksack looks a better quality than you get round here. And his clothes look, I don't know, expensive, but different somehow."

"You're right, he's a nifty dresser."

"Definitely foreign, Dad."

"No." Billy frowned. "There's something familiar about the cut of his jib. Something about the way he stands, so straight. He reminds me of . . ." he shook his head as memory remained elusive. Then he looked at her and said emphatically, "Bet he was in the army!"

"Navy!"

They often played this game, trying by observation, to decide who and what the visitors were and occasionally, Billy saw them in The Pirate, and either confirmed or disproved their wild guesses. Lydia went up to respond to yet another call from her mother, content that she had teased her father out of his misery.

Once lunch was over, Lydia slipped out to spend a couple of hours with Molly. She walked along the seafront, pushing her way through a crowd of people who had just alighted from a coach and were looking about them in a bemused way.

She saw the man again, still looking towards the castle ruin high on its hill beyond the shops. She changed direction slightly and walked closer to him. With people from the coach trip still hovering, undecided on which way to walk, it was easy to stand and study him without him being aware of her scrutiny.

He was younger than she had first thought. Probably middle thirties. He was tall and strongly built, with dark, reddish hair that was worn longer than normal for someone so formally dressed. His eyes, as he stared over the heads of the crowd towards the ruined castle, were hooded and dark and his face was deeply tanned.

"He hasn't been holidaying here, then!" Molly laughed when they met a few minutes later. "Rust more like with the summer we've had!"

Molly was the same height as Lydia and her colouring was similar but they were not alike. Molly was plump, and wore clothes which emphasised her fullness. Tight-fitting tops, short, straight skirts and a deeply cinched waist.

The girls were unalike in character as well as looks, Lydia being a quiet, gentle girl who constantly stepped back to allow her friend any limelight. Molly was first to put herself forward, always ready for adventure or laughter, both of which she was currently finding in the arms of her secret lover. The fun was mostly in avoiding being found out, she had little to lose except a reputation, which at the tender age of twenty-two, seemed hardly worth a moment's thought, apart from the opinion of Mr and Mrs Frank with whom she shared a home.

Molly's eyes glittered with excitement and Lydia guessed her friend's thoughts were on the next meeting with her lover.

The man who had been looking up at the castle, had picked up his kitbag and canvas holdall and turned away from the seashore. He pushed his way through the crowd and went to find a hotel.

He was tired, having been travelling for several days and he intended to eat and then sleep until the following morning. Tomorrow he would look out a few remembered faces, see if anyone remembered him and if they did, whether they would give him the time of day. He chuckled, his sombre eyes softening momentarily. Not many would welcome him back if they remembered the way he'd been as a boy!

It was such a long time ago, and memories of the wild, seventeen year old boy he had then been, were probably softened by time, into nothing more than juvenile stupidity.

Later that day, Molly was waiting for her date at the top of the lane where small fishermen's cottages led up onto the steep hill. They did not exchange affectionate greetings when he arrived, but walked rather sedately on up the hill. Turning off onto a narrow footpath, they were soon hidden by the gorse and brambles and goat-willow which clothed the hillside. Further on were the half-demolished remains of army huts abandoned after the war and a sheltered place for lovers to meet. It was only then that they kissed and revealed the fact that they were lovers.

"Did you have a job getting out today, love?" he asked, as they entered their regular shelter.

"No, but Lydia's guessed I meet someone every Sunday evening besides during the week when you can get away. I don't think she knows who though, yet. We'll have to be careful."

"D'you think we should give it a miss for a week or so, until her curiosity has faded, then?"

"Why not go back to our usual place to meet? Not much chance of anyone seeing us there, is there?"

"You mean the castle grounds?" he frowned.

"Closed it is, except to people like us who can get in through the woods or clamber over the gate. No one is likely to see us there."

Between love-making and tender talk which both enjoyed but neither believed, they decided to make the castle grounds on a Tuesday evening their new arrangement. Leaving her at the corner of the lane, the man gave her a kiss and hurried off to join his friends for a game of cards. Friends who unwittingly gave him an alibi of sorts if his wife became suspicious and questioned his absence.

Molly returned to the house where she lived with Mr and Mrs Frank and began to prepare supper. She no longer acted as a lodger, but had gradually taken over the running of the house. She was very fond of them; they were the nearest thing to parents she had ever known. Her own mother and father had abandoned her when she was still very young. She had shared rooms and various lodgings, even staying with Lydia for a while, until Annie had objected.

Mr and Mrs Frank did not know about her affair and she hoped they wouldn't until it either ended or

30

came out into the open, which would only happen if her lover decided to leave his wife and marry her. Even then she would make sure they understood she would never leave them. The elderly couple had promised that the house would be hers after their death if she would stay with them and look after them. But that wasn't the reason she didn't want them upset. She did not want them living in fear of her leaving them. She loved them too much to do that. And they were important enough for her to want them to live for many more years.

But she was beginning to feel less than happy about the secret affair. She had told Lydia she was better off without Glyn that there were better ways to live than as an appendage to a man, but she was no longer being truthful when she insisted it was not what she wanted.

She set the table with cold meats and salad and a plate of bread and butter cut thinly, just the way they liked it. The Franks wouldn't eat much of it, but she always did her best to make what she offered them as attractive as she could.

She had planned surprises for them too. A visit from an old friend, when they mentioned they would like to see him again, a trip to the cinema with Howe's taxis taking them there and back. A special tea on their forty-fourth anniversary, with flowers and a specially ordered cake. All this occupied her mind but she was restless.

Her emotions were taking control; the love affair, entered upon so casually was becoming more and more important to her. It was no longer easy to treat her boyfriend as unimportant and trivial.

Her words to Lydia about avoiding commitments and having fun, were beginning to have a hollow ring.

She spent time imagining how it would be if he could be persuaded to leave his wife and marry her. For the first time since the affair began, she wanted to discuss her situation with someone. Throwing off her apron, she hurried through the quiet streets to the house with its view across the bay and asked Lydia to go with her for a walk.

"Give me a moment to finish sewing in this sleeve," Lydia said, sensing the urgency of her friend's need to talk. "If Mam's asleep I might sneak out for half an hour. Dad's in The Pirate with Gimlet and the others and won't be back for a while." Hurriedly repacking the sewing tin and making sure her mother was sleeping, the two girls set off to walk along the dark streets of the silent village. Only from the public houses came signs that not everyone was at home. The lights shone brightly from the windows and spilled out from the door as people went in and out. Occasional laughter rang out and, to Molly in her restless mood the sound added to her melancholy.

"My friend and I have been lovers for almost a year," Molly began.

"Wasting your youth you are. Why do you bother with him, Molly?"

"He's unhappy with his wife."

"Don't they all say that? Not much of a reason to fritter away your life on him."

"It happens to be true."

"They all say that too."

"Oh, all right, if you aren't going to even listen!" Molly turned and began to walk back the way they had come.

"Sorry. I'll hear you out before I say another word. Right?"

"She was expecting a baby, see, and they got

married because it was the right thing to do. Then only weeks after the wedding, the baby, well, she lost it. So there they were, married and not even liking each other, hating each other for being trapped in a marriage neither wanted. They'd never loved each other."

"How can you make a baby without feeling love for each other?" Lydia asked quietly.

"It happens. Men will take what's on offer without thinking further ahead than the next five minutes. Oh, yes. Women too! Sex is wonderful, as you'll find out when your Mr Right comes along, but I take your point. Without love it isn't so special. There's the aftermath of guilt, see, which you don't get if you're in love."

"Do you feel guilt? Loving him and knowing he has a wife?"

"It's no longer a game of gratification. I – I think I love him. I want him to leave his wife." She stared at her friend to see her reaction. "Is that very wicked, Lydia?"

"D'you think he will?"

"Of course he *wants* to. But with his mam and dad hounding him and trying to make him behave as they think he should, it's difficult for him. I can see that."

"And you, could you live with the pointing fingers and being shunned by so-called friends? Even in this day and age, people criticize women accused of breaking up marriages. Most women feel vulnerable and they shout quick when it happens to someone else, fearing it might be their turn next."

"I don't want it made public yet. I don't want anything to frighten Mr and Mrs Frank into thinking I'll leave them. I won't. I promised them I'd stay with them until they pass peacefully away and look after them properly until they do and I'll keep that promise. They've been good to me and I wouldn't let them down, not even for – for 'what's-his-name', my fella. But seeing me mixed up in a divorce might make them worry and I don't want that, I love them, see. So there you are, a fine ol' mess, for sure. Me wanting him to leave his wife but not wanting anyone to breathe a word in case Mr and Mrs Frank are upset."

Lydia was silent for a while.

"Lydia?" Molly coaxed.

"I keep thinking of how I would feel if I had married Glyn and he'd found someone else. It's humiliating enough having Glyn leave me for this 'Cath' woman. And we weren't even officially engaged."

"No good talking to you then is it!" Molly again turned and this time ran from her friend down past the shops towards the sea. She stopped as Lydia caught her up and held her arm. "I know it will cause misery," she sighed, her voice trembling tearfully. "But I love him and want him and I know we'd be happy."

"You don't want it out in the open anyway, not yet, so I suggest you stop meeting for a while, let things calm down. You've been seen walking up past the fishermen's cottages so it won't be long before you – and he – are recognised. Stay away from him for a while to see how you both feel. That's my advice, if you want it. That way you won't risk upsetting Mr and Mrs Frank and if the marriage *is* mended, well, best you know now, before wasting any more of your time."

"I can't do that, but we've chosen a different place to meet, where we shouldn't be seen."

"If you must continue to meet, then good. Just don't tell anyone where or when."

*　　*　　*

34

The tall man had to get into the castle. It had been sheer luck that he had heard that the place was closing for repairs. Just when everything was looking so good this had to come back and haunt him. He had to find what he had hidden and remove it to a place where it would never be found. He was angry with himself. He should have done something before this.

He had been watching for several days and knew that children still managed to get not only into the grounds, but inside the castle itself. He had heard them laughing and running about and guessed at the games they were playing. He had seen the plans for the work that would be done and although it seemed unlikely that his secret would be discovered, he had to go and move the items and take them far away, this time making sure they would never again see the light of day. Weighted down and dropped overboard from a small boat, that was the best solution. But first he had to find them. Would he remember the exact spot, or would his memory let him down?

The following Tuesday, Molly set off to the woods on the sea side of the castle. A terrace of small houses – one of which belonged to the Howes – ran along the road facing the sea, and behind them a path ran between houses and the tree-covered slope. A track led up through a strip of woodland to the castle mound. A sea mist was adding to the chill of the October evening. It was dark once she left the lights along the road, but nevertheless, she kept to the shadows as she worked her way around between the backs of houses and the beginning of the wood.

The trees made strange shapes that seemed to move as she passed them. Leaves touched her face and branches of straggly brambles caught at her trousers and pulled her back. Trying to walk without making a sound added to her fear, the small noises she did make frightening her. The castle loomed up into the sky as she climbed the grassy mound, black and very different from its day-time tranquillity. She was relieved when she finally stood near the corner of the building which had once been the chapel.

Following the high walls, she worked her way blindly, feeling the walls for guidance, nervous now there was no light at all to guide her to the next corner. There a window had been weakened by the regular visits of Neville Nolan and his gang and she stopped and waited for her man-friend to arrive.

The path at this point was narrow, reduced in width by a stream of water coming from the castle wall that had weakened the earth causing it to slide down occasionally to rest against the allotment fence. The blackness of the night got to her and she couldn't stay there listening for him.

The path was hardly wide enough for her to walk and she sidled sideways, her back to the walls, moving around towards the gateway, where once a portcullis had protected it from invasion. The silence was palpable, the night air pressing in on her, clammy and still and seeming to hum in her ears. Her heart was racing as she stood expecting to hear a sound that threatened her. But with what she hadn't any idea, it was just that the night seemed to crackle with danger.

This wasn't a good idea. Why hadn't she insisted he met her on the road below and walked with her through this eerie place? Bravado had made her laugh when he had suggested it. Now she regretted her confidence. She decided that in future she would arrange to meet him where there was some light, and they would walk through the trees and around the walls together. Adventure or not, this was definitely the last time.

As she reached the corner where, at each side of the gateway, the walls recessed for towers which had never been built, she gave a small sigh of relief. At least there were distant lights, the shops along the road giving out a glow, and there was the sound of people and cars passing not far away. More confident now, but still intending to make this the last time, she stepped into the tower recess and a figure appeared and stopped right in front of her; big, threatening and too close for her to run.

Afterwards, she thought he had been as startled at the confrontation as she, but at the moment it was all her nightmares and fear reaching fruition at once. She attempted to scream but the push he gave her sent her sliding then falling, off the path, down through the undergrowth which hid a steep bank, until she came to a stop, unharmed but breathless and terribly afraid, near the fence of the allotments.

She held her breath and listened but there wasn't a sound. Where was he, the man who attacked her? And where was her boyfriend? Why wasn't he rushing to help? She stood up and pressed herself into a blackthorn bush unaware of the discomfort of the prickly branches, and stared, wide-eyed, around her. The light coming from the road was limited but she could make out the dark towering walls of the castle above her.

Then the faint light from the street lamps began to fade as rain began to fall, softly, with a gentle hiss that obliterated all sound. Where was he, this hooligan who had frightened her? Was he still up there watching her, waiting for her to move? Intending to push her again? Only this time to wait until she was near the high wall from where he could push her down onto the road far below? Afraid to move, shivering with the chill of the rain that was slowly soaking her right through, she listened, half imagining she could hear his breathing above the softly falling rain.

After an age, she moved out of the shadows and, slowly at first, then at a low, scuttling run, hurried down the grassy slope towards the gate opposite Stella's house. The castle gate was locked as she knew it would be but nothing would persuade her to go back through the wood. Having to climb the gate made her utter small squeaks of fear, expecting at every moment the man to reappear and attack her.

Then she heard footsteps running towards her. She felt her fingers weaken, the muscles in her legs failed her and she fell back from the gate and prepared to run, not thinking where, just running from whatever new danger threatened.

"Molly? Is that you, love?"

"Thank goodness!" she sobbed. "Where have you been? Why were you so late? There's a man . . . and he pushed me, and . . ." Explanations were muffled as she clung to him across the metal barrier. Then he was over the gate in a leap and holding her trembling body to his own. She smelled of damp earth and rotting leaves.

"Come on, love. Whoever he is he'll be well gone now. Some idiot of a tramp most likely, frightening you away from the spot he'd chosen for the night." He helped her over the gate, concern for her fright making him careless of being seen, and talking soothingly, began to walk her home.

"Molly?" Lydia stepped out of a shop doorway

where she had been admiring some shoes, and bumped into her friend. For one heart-stopping moment she thought Molly's companion, with his arms draped so affectionately around her shoulders was Glyn. Then she realised it was Glyn's brother. So Tomos was Molly's secret lover. No wonder she wanted to keep his identity a secret!

"Tomos! So you are the married man who's wife doesn't love him? Molly, how could you?"

"Please, Lydia, keep it to yourself," Tomos pleaded, after trying in vain to bluff it out. "All right, we've been seeing each other for a year, what can you tell us that we haven't already said ourselves a thousand times? Melanie and I have never loved each other, you know that's true. We both know our marriage was a mistake."

"Please, Lydia, we don't want it all to come out now, not like this."

Molly explained about the attack and gradually Lydia's outrage cooled. "You could at least be honest enough to tell her," she said. "Others will soon know."

Lydia was shocked. It was one thing to share the secret of a love affair but very different when you knew and liked the unsuspecting wife. How could she keep quiet and watch Melanie being cheated?

"We will tell Melanie, and soon," Tomos said, "but not now. Please, keep quiet for a little while longer? Let me tell her when the moment is right?"

After a lot of persuading, Lydia gave her word. She was still raw with the unhappiness of Glyn telling her he had found someone else and knowing Tomos's parents and his wife made her more sensitive than she might otherwise have been. "I won't cover for you, mind," she said firmly. "Not like I did the day you pretended to go home with a bilious attack." She saw from Molly's expression that her guess had been correct. "I'll keep quiet because it's best for Melanie to hear about this from you, Tomos. But don't even think of asking me to be your alibi because that is something I will not do."

After the frightening experience in the castle grounds, which had resulted in their being seen by Lydia, Tomos and Molly continued to meet there, although Molly would never venture alone further than the gate, which was near Lydia's Auntie Stella's. There the street lights and the activity around the fish and chip shop on the main road at least gave them warning of someone approaching. Together, Molly clinging to him nervously, they would walk up through the allotments over a weakened section of fence. They would make their way to their favourite place at the back of the castle behind the chapel block and snuggle against its walls in precious privacy.

One evening Tomos arrived early. His wife, Melanie had gone to the pictures and he slipped in via the wood and wandered around the castle looking for a way inside. He saw that he could gain access through a window which had been carelessly blocked. With little trouble, he pushed some of rocks aside and widened the hole which, he guessed, was regularly used by children.

Although she was afraid, Molly wouldn't show it: she was the "bit of fun", wasn't she? Always ready for laughter and adventure, taking on any 'dare'. Not the established and complaisant wife! With encouragement and stifled laughter they went inside and found a room with the roof intact. It smelled unpleasantly of dampness and other indistinguishable odours but it promised a winter of, if not comfort, at least shelter from the wind and rain and, with the public forbidden entry, blessed privacy.

"Thank goodness Lydia promised to keep our secret," Molly said. "At least she's the only one who knows." In this, however, she was wrong.

Gimlet was fuming. He went round to Billy Jones's house and stumped up the stairs from the kitchen without waiting for an invitation. "Talked about, we are, and all because of that stupid son of mine."

"Which one?" Billy asked, offering him a chair.

Gimlet was too angry to sit, he paced up and down the room glaring at the walls as if the blame was written across them. "That damned stupid Tomos of course! Only gone and found himself another woman, hasn't he!"

"Never!"

"And his little wife Melanie sitting at home embroidering pillowcases for when they get a place of their own. What are we going to do, Billy?"

"We?" Billy chuckled. "*We*? Nothing to do with me, and glad I am to say it."

"I want to give him a real fright, got any ideas?"

"Tell him you've let his room and want him out?" Billy suggested. "I've always thought your Mary has made them too comfortable, mind."

"You've got to help me, Billy. Imagine what it's like me having to face his poor wife knowing what I know. Terrible it is."

"What can I do?" Billy asked in exasperation.

"They're meeting at the castle tonight and I thought we'd arrange a sort of welcoming committee. I want to warn them off and I don't want to be overheard. The fewer that find out the better. Facing them in their little 'love nest' will be more of a shock. But

41

first I thought we'd have a bit of fun. You with me, boy?" When he explained what he had planned, Billy nodded agreement.

"Too good to miss," he smiled. "We aren't too old for a bit of a lark!"

Tomos and Molly weren't meeting at the castle that Tuesday evening. Melanie had gone to visit her mother in Cardiff for a few days, and they were making the most of their unexpected freedom. They were going to town to see a film and pretend for a while that they were a normal, happy, courting couple.

Two hours later, while Tomos and Molly were happily enjoying the comfort of sitting in the warm, dark cinema with their arms around each other, Gimlet and Billy were shivering with the cold, waiting in the castle for them to appear. Fortunately the night was clear and dry. Between them the men carried a couple of sheets and several torches with which they planned to frighten the couple, have a bit of a laugh before revealing themselves, sharply changing the mood to one of seriousness and warning them that their secret was well and truly out.

Unaware they they were being watched by a group of small boys led by Neville Nolan, they practiced opening the sheets and covering their heads with them, using the torches held in their mouths to light the apparitions, planning the unearthly moans.

As they were so engaged, the boys, who had entered the castle close behind them with the ease of regular practise, crept up behind them and, while they were ensconced in the sheets, touched them and whispered a low moaning wail in their ears.

Leaping up, frantically trying to escape from the clinging folds, dropping the torches and bumping into each other, the two men finally extricated themselves and ran to where they had entered, and, each trying to be first, made their escape.

As the first conspirator reached the ground he was hit severely across his head. When Gimlet finally managed, with fumbling fingers, to find the spare torch, he discovered that Billy was unconscious and bleeding from a head wound.

Chapter Three

Leaving Billy on the ground with a coat thrown over him and a torch, lit, near his hand, Gimlet ran to the gate, vaulted over it like a two year old and rushed to knock on Stella's door. Although it had been a serious attack, Gimlet did not want the police involved.

"Just go and phone for Glyn, will you?" he asked the bemused lady. "Best I go back and wait with Billy." He explained where he would be and ran back to sit beside Billy who was sitting up looking around and wondering what had happened.

After the phone box call to Howe's Taxis to explain to Glyn that his father needed him at the castle, Stella called on Lydia to tell her Billy was hurt. Lydia insisted on coming at once.

Her mother's reaction was to begin to sob and cry and demand sleeping tablets to shut out the pain.

"Mam," Lydia patiently explained, "I've got to go and see to Dad. You'll have to stay awake until I get back. You'll want to know how he is, won't you?"

"I can't face it. You'll have to go for the doctor."

"No, you don't need the doctor, not this time. Dad's been attacked and I have to go."

"You don't understand," wailed Annie. She crawled from her bed and took sleeping tablets as soon as Lydia closed the door behind her.

Lydia and Stella hurried back through the dark

streets, each wondering if they should stop at the police station but agreeing that, until they knew exactly what had happened, they were wisest to do as Gimlet asked and avoid telling anyone.

Lydia was shocked when she saw her father's face and she gasped before preparing to ask the obvious, "What happened?"

"Don't ask," was Billy's mournful greeting. "One minute we were climbing down from the castle window and the next Gimlet tripping over me, then there was poor me on the floor and out as cold as a fish on a slab and now I'm as giddy as a ten-pint jelly. And neither of us knows what happened."

"What were you doing in the castle at this time of night for heaven's sake!"

"Oh, it was all a bit of a lark," Billy hedged, glancing at Gimlet.

Lydia took the bowl of water and bandages which Stella had brought and began bathing her father's face. He appeared to have fallen flat on his face, the skin was grazed and bruises were already darkening his chin, nose and forehead. On the back of his head was a frighteningly large swelling, which he was refusing to explain. She was so intent on her father's injuries she hardly noticed the presence of Glyn. When he spoke she was surprised at his presence.

"Sorry your father was hurt, Lydia," Glyn said, stepping towards her. "What were the daft pair doing?"

"I don't know, but I'm not moving from here until we're told!" she said firmly.

He took the bowl from her and took it back to the kitchen. "I've put the kettle on for more tea, I think we could do with it, while we wait for the explanation," he said.

"Best we tell them, Gimlet," Billy muttered and Gimlet nodded solemnly.

They waited until the tea was poured, then, in sepulchral tones Billy tried to explain that they were preparing to be ghosts. "I found out that Tomos has a girlfriend. Sneaking about seeing another women he is, while his poor wife sits at home trusting him." He looked at Glyn and the others to see how they were taking the news.

"We thought we'd have a bit of fun, you know, frighten them a bit then get serious and give them a lecture."

"But it was you two who had the fright?" As the explanations became more detailed under questioning, Glyn's serious expression collapsed and he and Lydia shared a grin which exploded into laughter which was partly relief and partly pure merriment.

"Really, Dad, what a stupid thing to do!" Lydia tried to scold but failed to stop giggling.

When the laughter had subsided, Billy said quietly, "Fools we were for sure, but what puzzles me and Gimlet, is this. What reason would someone have to discourage us from going into the castle?"

"It was kids surely?"

"Kids it was who frightened us, and serve us both right for that, mind. But this slap on the head, now," he touched his bandaged head carefully, "this wasn't the work of no kids, was it? Someone doesn't want us around the castle."

"I think we should tell the police," Stella said. "Whatever reason they had for being there, it couldn't have been an honest one if they did that to poor Billy." She touched his head, adjusted the bandage, obviously anxious about him. But she spoke briskly when she added, "Silly fools you were, the pair of you."

Billy began to shake his head, but groaned as it began to hurt.

"No, Stella," Gimlet said urgently. "Please, let's keep this to ourselves. I wouldn't want to explain, not about Molly and – he stopped and looked at Glyn and Lydia.

"All right, we'll say nothing about that fool of a brother of mine." Glyn spoke with obvious disapproval, but he agreed with the others that perhaps it was wisest to forget the incident. "But," he added, if there's any more trouble up there, I'll change my mind and go straight to the police. Right?"

"If there's more trouble up at that damned castle, we won't be involved, for sure!" Billy replied, "Eh, Gimlet?"

"We'll be keeping well clear!"

The two men looked so serious that Lydia and Glyn shared another smile at the thought of their fathers playing at ghosts.

When they reached home, it was Glyn who helped Billy into his chair. He stood uneasily at the window, and Lydia asked, "Stay for a moment, will you, just while I see to Mam and get Dad a cup of tea."

"Something stronger wouldn't go amiss," Billy muttered, but before Lydia could take a breath to argue, he had fallen asleep and was soon gently snoring.

During the first few moments Glyn was there, Annie called down three times for some trivial thing. On the third occasion he put out an arm to stop her from running up to see what her mother wanted. He smiled and held out his hand to her.

"Come on, Lydia, you need·a break from this, you've had a nasty shock. We'll go and find a late night café and share a pot of tea."

47

"But I can't leave Dad, and—"

"We're going out for half an hour, Missus Jones," he called up the stairs. "Keep an eye on your Billy, will you?" Covering Lydia's ears against Annie's tearful protests, he hurried her out.

"What do you think really happened at the castle tonight?" Lydia asked, when they were seated and had been served with their tea and hot buttered toast.

"Your father is right, it wasn't the work of that little menace Neville Nolan and his gang. Someone wanted to make sure no one else went wandering around the castle at night. First Molly being pushed, now your father."

"You knew before then? About your brother and Molly?"

"That your friend is deliberately breaking up Tomos and Melanie's marriage, yes, I know."

"Molly is fully responsible is it? Not Tomos too?"

"Flattered he is that a girl like that would be interested in him."

"Could someone be watching them and trying to make Tomos behave? Frighten them off? After all, that was what your father was trying to do. Some relation of Melanie perhaps? Trying to make her husband behave?"

"There's no way your dad and mine could be mistaken for Tomos and Molly. No, I think this is something else. Perhaps we can put our heads together and find out what. But," he added firmly as she began to agree, "you must promise me you won't go near that castle on your own, even during the day."

Wondering if he still cared or was simply mouthing platitudes, Lydia smiled but didn't give her word.

Sitting at a table behind them and unnoticed by

the couple, a young man watched them with interest. He was trying to work out who they were. They were obviously uneasy with each other even though they were deep in conversation. He was puzzled. Did they know each other well or were they strangers learning about one another? He saw the man's hand reach over to touch the girl's arm and smiled as she pulled it away. A lovers' quarrel. No doubt about it.

He leaned their way, about to speak but changed his mind and moved slightly, hoping to overhear something of their conversation. The girl was a good looker and he might be willing to do some consoling if they were saying goodbye.

Since Glyn and Lydia had cancelled their plans to marry, they had seldom met. Both seemed afraid to look at each other and perhaps reveal the strong affection that still simmered beneath the surface. Now, with the accident in which both of their fathers were involved having brought them together, they were in no hurry to separate. Glyn ordered a fresh pot of tea and Lydia was content to sit and talk.

Gradually, they relaxed and sank into their previous companionship, although Lydia was wary not to be seduced into believing they could ever return to the love they had once shared and which she had thought would last all their lives.

"When are you going to London? It is London where Cath lives, isn't it?" she forced herself to ask.

"Oh, some time next month I think. It might be longer, after Christmas maybe. Cath is looking for accommodation and it isn't easy."

"No, of course not."

Glyn turned back to her and stared into her eyes. "Until then, I'll be very busy," he said as if forcing her to believe him. "I'm going to concentrate on building up Tomos's business for him. I'll have plenty to keep me occupied, stop me from feeling lonely."

Hot with anger and humiliation, Lydia stood up, scraping back her chair and reaching for her coat. "You don't have to spell it out as if I'm a simpleton, Glyn Howe! I'm not looking to come back into your life. No, thank you. Cath is welcome to you! Ending our engagement was the best thing to happen to me and it's something I'll never regret. Never!" She hurried from the cafe, but not so hastily she might give the impression she was hiding tears. She stopped at the doorway, turned and said calmly, "Stay away from me and if you want something to fill your time and stop you feeling lonely, while you sit and wait for Cath to organise your life for you, try and persuade that stupid brother of yours to stay away from Molly. Trouble you are the pair of you!"

"Ex-girlfriend I gather," the man at the other table said with a smile. "Sorry, but it was impossible not to guess what was happening."

"Don't worry. I don't suppose it matters who heard us," Glyn said without looking at the man.

"What was that about the castle? I understand it's closed?"

"I haven't a clue, mate, ring the Guildhall, they'll tell you." Glyn's irritability showed. He shouldn't have tried to be clever with Lydia, trying to hint that he was going to be too busy, warning her off. Now he'd lost the chance of them being friends, and it would be ages before she would talk to him.

"Glyn Howe isn't it?" the man said.

Glyn seemed not to hear. Without adding further to the conversation, he went out.

* * *

50

Billy didn't go out for several days after the blow on the head and when he did, it was with Gimlet. The two friends walked along the foreshore, towards The Pirate, watching the sea in its winter mood with a full tide surging and boiling, touching the top of the sea wall. The man on whom Billy and Lydia had been making observations some days previously was sitting on a bench staring up at the castle. Around him men were busy working on boats; cleaning, repairing, painting, putting them away like expensive toys, until spring.

"Seen that chap around, have you, Gimlet?" Billy asked. "Lydia and I had a game trying to guess who he was. I thought he must have been in the army." He must have been talking louder than he realised, because the young man turned his head and stared at them. Then he walked over and Billy backed away, touching his injured head nervously, half expecting the man to complain about his nosiness, but as the man drew near he smiled.

"Did I hear you say Gimlet? Would you be Gilbert Howe?"

"I am, yes, and this is—"

"Billy Jones?" The man laughed at their puzzled expression, his deep-set eyes secretive in the tanned face. "You don't remember me, I was only seventeen when you saw me last. Matthew Hiatt." He held out a hand. "Rosie Hiatt's young brother. You might have forgotten me, but you can't have forgotten my sister, Rosie. She disappeared sixteen years ago."

"No," Gimlet said shakily. "No, none of us have forgotten her." The three of them talked for a while but all the time, Gimlet was trying to get away and think. Rosie Hiatt's brother, back after all these years. He wondered what he could want. Surely he couldn't be hoping to find his sister after so much time had passed?

"Rosie lodged with you and your wife, didn't she?" Matthew asked and Gimlet was so lost in the surprise of the meeting, it was some time before he realised the question was addressed to him.

"Oh, yes, she did. Damn it all, I can't believe you're that seventeen year old Matthew Hiatt."

"I'm not," Matthew said, and there was a sudden coldness in his dark, hooded eyes. "That Matthew Hiatt has gone forever. This Matthew Hiatt is older, wiser and determined to find out what happened to his sister." Matthew had no strong desire to learn of the fate of the sister he hardly remembered. If rumours were to be believed she was nothing but a tart, and she probably ran off to escape the fingernails of a jealous wife.

"I thought I recognised Glyn the other day, in the Surf café late one night," Matthew went on. "With a very pretty girl, lovely curls and big blue eyes. Sparking mad they were I remember."

"That might have been my daughter, Lydia," Billy said.

"Good heavens. Lydia? She's grown into a beauty. I don't think she was even in school when I left the village. I'll have to introduce myself."

Billy didn't reply. Anger flooded his still bruised and cut face, his swollen nose giving him a pugnacious expression. If even half the things Matthew Hiatt had been accused of all those years ago were true, then he didn't want Lydia going anywhere near him! A right tearaway he'd been.

Gimlet seemed unable to speak. He was staring at Matthew as if he'd seen a ghost. After so long, he hadn't expected to see Rosie Hiatt's brother return.

He'd found his feet by the look of him, good clothes and plenty of money to spend on buying drinks. He'd obviously made a good life for himself after such a bad start. He wondered why he'd returned, but daren't ask. Best he showed no interest in him at all.

Later that evening, Billy and Gimlet saw Matthew in The Pirate. Once people knew who he was, reminiscences flowed with the drink and the occasion of Matthew's reappearance seemed an excuse for celebration. Gimlet didn't want to stay, but Billy persuaded him and he agreed, not wanting to raise any curiosity over his reluctance to spend time with Matthew. Or talk about Rosie.

When closing time drew near, Matthew raised a glass and toasted, "Rosie Hiatt, wherever you may be." His companions solemnly echoed his words, and Billy puzzled briefly over the discomfiture showing on the face of Gimlet Howe. Why should his friend be worried if he wasn't? It was so long ago, and no one would remember.

Molly was well contented with the fun of a secret affair with Tomos but increasingly she has begun to hope that it would lead to something permanent. Although Gimlet and Glyn knew about the affair nothing had been said once the warning had been given on the night of the attack. She knew Gimlet wanted them to end it but Tomos showed no sign of following his father's wishes.

They remembered with glee Gimlet and Billy's attempts to haunt the castle, and only sobered when they began to wonder who had struck Billy such a blow that he had fallen from the high window.

"Perhaps we aren't the only ones to use the castle for our assignation," Tomos said.

"Assignation, how romantic, Tomos." Molly smiled. "But if it was someone wanting privacy, they've got it. We won't be going there again, will we?"

"No?" Tomos asked provocatively. "Not scared are you?"

"Not if you're with me, love."

"You're such fun, Molly and it's fun I've missed with Melanie. I can't imagine her facing the dark ruined castle for a few minutes of my company."

"It'll be fun to go there and wonder if we're being watched, or whether we're disturbing another couple's evening by our intrusion."

"You really would go there again?"

"I think it would be a laugh, don't you?" If Tomos wanted to risk another visit to the castle, she wouldn't refuse.

Sex was usually blamed for a man seeking other delights but sex wasn't always the purpose of their sometimes brief meetings. Tomos would talk and explain about his empty marriage and the futility of keeping up a pretence. She would discuss her affection for the Franks and her worries about their occasional health problems.

"If it wasn't for Mam and Dad insisting I stay, I'd be out of that house and into a place with you before you could say yes or no!" Tomos said one evening.

"Oh, Tomos, it's a wonderful dream. Perhaps, one day we'll make it come true?"

"In the meantime we'll add a bit of spice to our lives and go back to meeting at the castle, if you really dare," Tomos smiled. "This time we'll take a couple of blankets, shall we? The mud up there is difficult to explain when I get home!"

Access was easy via the window, and Tomos promised to take in a couple of torches and a few blankets. They thought they'd be safe from observation by Neville Nolan's gang. The boys no longer used the area for their games, warned off perhaps by their parents. Certainly Gimlet and Billy would think twice about following them there. As for the person who attacked Billy, they tried to convince themselves that he would not risk returning.

Lydia was going to her aunt's house one evening to collect a knitted pram set which she had made and which Stella had sewn up for her. It was late and although the evening was cold, the air was cleanly crisp and the sky looked newly washed, with an almost full moon and bright stars, and it was pleasant to stroll on the quiet streets. As she turned the corner and came in sight of her aunt's gateway she saw Molly walking across the road to stand at the corner further along the lane than Stella's house. What could she be doing out so late? Surely she and Tomos weren't still using the castle for their meetings? She knew they were still seeing each other, although Molly refused to discuss it.

She looked up at the towering walls, huge in the deceiving light of the moon and the distorting shadows. Allowing her imagination full rein she saw faces at the windows and people standing on the battlements, which she knew were only dappled shadows and tendrils of ivy but which frightened her nevertheless. How could they go there and sit and talk and kiss and not be aware of the atmosphere of danger it must surely hold? She knew she couldn't go in there, not for anything.

She was unashamedly curious and went to stand at her aunt's gate. Tomos appeared soon after and slipped an arm around Molly's shoulder. They must be keeping to the lanes, or perhaps they had found a place in the old lime kiln in the woods. But no, they climbed the gate with ease and walked up the steep grassy slope to the gateway of the castle.

Lydia shuddered at the thought. At least she and Glyn had been able to sit in the warmth and comfort of her parents' kitchen. Thoughts of Glyn and the evenings they had spent beside the small fireplace which heated the domestic water, saddened her. She tried to convince herself that she was better off than Molly, who loved a man who wasn't free, but the melancholy the memories revived wouldn't go away.

Their laughter echoed back to where she stood and for a moment she was consumed with jealousy, an aching wish that it was she walking to a castle rendezvous with Glyn. But then a shadow passed over the moon, momentarily blotting out all but the faintest reflection of the building in the starlight and she told herself that nothing, not even Glyn, could make her face that.

Inside the castle, the moonlight transformed the place into a stage-set. The first character was already playing his part. A tall man was pacing around in the area that had once been the kitchens.

The three huge fireplaces were still there, with the wide chimneys reaching up to the highest part of the curtain wall. There was no roof but much of the stone walls remained. He moved to the fireplace in the centre of the long wall where he was shadowed from the surprisingly bright moonlight. Swiftly and silently he measured and marked places with some short bamboo canes he had brought, concentrating on his task, forcing memory to assist him. For the third undisturbed night he had lifted several areas of turf and dug out shallow pits in the hope of finding what he had buried so long ago. He worked methodically, each night's digging marked with the sticks, which he took away with him at the end of his session. So far there had been nothing but a few coins, cigarette packets, an earring and, unbelievably, some bicycle clips.

He wasn't too disappointed when, having dug as deeply as he planned, he had failed to find anything. He was almost certain he was still too far from the steps leading to the battlements. Starting further over was a precaution. He didn't want to have to go back over where he had searched and start poking about like a crazy mole. This way he would cover the ground methodically and thoroughly and be certain to find what he was looking for without too much disturbance.

He took a long time replacing the turves. The neater it was done the sooner the scars of his search would fade. Thank goodness there was plenty of rain in this area. It would soon re-settle and by the time work was due to start, in April, no one would know it had been disturbed. The second pit was covered as neatly as possible and he raised his spade to begin a third. He was so intent on his task that the sound of voices didn't penetrate for a moment. When it did he swore angrily. A woman's voice. A man's. Laughter. He gave a growl of rage and stepped back into the shadow of the wall.

What more would he have to do to make people stay away? He remembered the night when he had come upon the two men suddenly as they climbed out of the window, and hitting out at one of them in pure panic in fear of being seen and recognised. He

57

was glad he had taken the precaution of preparing another trap. He felt reasonably certain these present nuisances wouldn't go to the police. Knowing who they were, he doubted if they would want to report a fall of rocks in a place where they had no right to be, and in the wrong company.

They had to be using the window, the same way he had entered. If it was Tomos Howe and that girl, he would have at least an hour before they were ready to leave. With short footsteps he glided along keeping to the walls, moving like a wraith in the eerie light of the moon. The window by which they entered had a pile of rock below it. A wall had collapsed and by moving some of the smaller rocks and reinforcing the pile, Neville Nolan and his gang had created a pathway to make access and exit easy.

The tall man had removed and rebuilt it, spending three back-breaking nights on the job. Now, once he was up on the sill of the window, he only had to heave a couple of pieces of wood out of place and the lot tumbled, leaving no easy way for anyone inside the castle to get out.

In the small area that had once been the Chapel block, Tomos groaned and began kissing Molly again. The clear night had made it unnecessary to go into one of the dark rooms. Although the night was cold, the blankets added to their comfort and made lying together in the moonlight a delightful experience.

"Shall we still do this occasionally, when we're together for good?" Molly asked. "There's no need to forget what its like to make love out in the open, looking up at the moon."

"I wouldn't mind living in a tent and making love under the stars just to be with you, love," Tomos said.

"Oh Tomos, I'm so impatient, but for both our sakes we have to wait. For you and Melanie this isn't the time, is it? There has to be the right moment. You have to give her time to find a new life, accept that you and she are finished, let her bow out gracefully."

"It's hard, love, but yes, we have to be patient. I just hope that no one else finds out about us before we're ready to announce our plans. I know it's soft, but I hope Melanie leaves me. That way I wouldn't feel we're building our happiness on someone else's sorrow."

"Fat chance," she sighed. "Who'd be daft enough to let you go?" She kissed him lightly and stood up. "Let's walk up to the battlements and look out over the sea. It must be beautiful now with a high tide and the moon full."

Tomos folded the blankets, threw them across his shoulder and, hand in hand, they stepped out of the doorway to walk along the open corridor towards the kitchen and the gateway, where stairs led up to the battlements.

"What was that?" Molly asked, clinging to him as a shadow passed in front of them.

"Only a cat or something," Tomos laughed. "Come on, don't tell me you're getting scared. We've been here for almost two hours and haven't heard a sound."

The stone steps, worn smooth by thousands of feet, curved upwards and soon they were standing above the arched gateway, looking out across the bay. It was almost as bright as day, the sea a shimmering pool with hardly a ripple of movement. The path of moonlight was faintly visible and seemed to lead their eyes on, beyond the horizon, a black line in the distance.

"It does look as if the world's flat, doesn't it?"

Tomos whispered. "Over there the saucer's edge which drops down into – what?"

"Don't, Tomos, you'll make me afraid."

"Go on with you! Nothing scares you!"

The rumble seemed far away at first, like a lorry making its way along the road far below them. Then it became louder as if something was approaching very fast. The noise was all around them and they couldn't guess the direction from which it came. They hugged each other from a danger they couldn't recognise. The tranquillity of the night had been torn apart. The roaring sound slowed to a trickle and stopped before they had time to work out what had caused it. They turned away from the calm sea and looked around the ground below them.

"Did we imagine that?" Tomos whispered into the still, silent night. Cautiously they made their way back through the open corridor, their hearts beating louder as they passed each doorway; their thoughts unformulated but half expecting something to jump out at them. The moonlight made the rooms even darker than usual, and they would have had to stand for a long time before their eyes became accustomed to the light, before they could investigate.

"We'll head straight back to the window and get out. Tomorrow will be plenty soon enough to find out what happened," Tomos whispered.

"It sounded like a wall falling, perhaps one of the areas they're meaning to repair," Molly whispered.

The tall man stood on the narrow path below the window, his outline misshapen amid the bare branches of an ash tree. He didn't hide, but listened as the footsteps approached the window inside the building. He heard the squeal of disappointment followed by the shout of anger when they realised their exit was blocked. He smiled as he heard their struggles to get up and reach the window. Perhaps now they'd be warned. He was satisfied that they couldn't get out, at least for some time. They would have to rebuild the pile of stones. He ran around the outer walls and skirting the open ground, ran to the bottom of the castle mound. He paused for a glance back and smiled before running on and slipping down through the woodland onto the road alongside the beach.

It was as she was leaving her aunt's house that Lydia heard the calls. "What's that?" she asked, turning her head to decide where the sounds were coming from. "Is it cats I can hear?"

"Cats indeed! There's someone in that castle again," Stella said. "I've heard noises coming from there several nights this week. Heaven alone knows what's going on up there. If the council want to close it why don't they make a proper job of it? Dangerous it is."

"Shall we call the police?" Lydia suggested. "If someone else has been hurt we can't ignore it, can we?"

"Best we have a look first. But then, how am I to get over the gate? You'll have to go, Lydia. Take a hammer for protection and my big torch." So an hour after deciding she could never visit the castle at night, Lydia had to change her mind. Hearing someone up there, obviously in trouble might have been sufficient to make her overcome her fear, but in addition, she knew without doubt that the person calling for help was Molly.

A man was approaching, coming from the direction of the main road and he stopped and called to them as Lydia was being helped up onto the gate. "Is something wrong?" he asked. "Can I help?"

"I . . . er . . ." Lydia hesitated. If it was Molly stuck up there, the fewer people who knew the better. But she looked up at the mysterious walls and valour failed her. She accepted his offer to go with her thankfully.

Stella wasn't so sure. "We don't know you, do we?" she said.

The man introduced himself. "I'm Matthew Hiatt," he told them. "I lived around here when I was a boy. I saw you in the Surf café with Glyn Howe. You're Billy Jones's daughter aren't you? I knew your father and his friend Gimlet Howe. They used to chase me for pinching apples out of Gimlet's back garden. And for other things as well! Did they mention meeting me a few days ago?"

"Matthew Hiatt?" Stella looked at him frowning. "Well I never! You're the brother of poor Rosie who disappeared all those years ago?"

"That's me. I'm just down here for a bit of a holiday. And you are—?"

"Stella Stevens. And this is my niece Lydia—"

"—Jones, Billy's daughter," Matthew interrupted with a smile. "Come on then, Lydia, before that poor woman up there loses her voice with shouting."

Stella offered them the use of a ladder and dropping it into the castle grounds, Matthew helped Lydia over the gate surprising her with the ease with which he lifted her, and they set off up the steep climb. With Matthew striding out beside her she felt the anxiety of approaching the castle at night slipping from her like a discarded cloak. A stranger, but one in whom she had confidence. The promise Glyn had asked her to make was forgotten.

Molly's calls were less frequent as the likelihood of being heard made her spirits flag, and it was Tomos whose voice led Lydia and Matthew to the window. Matthew was ignorant of the pathway and asked to hold Lydia's hand to be guided, a request to which she found no difficulty in acceeding.

Using the walls, out of which some stones protruded as a natural ladder, Matthew Hiatt reached the window and called to let the anxious couple know that help had arrived. Then leaving Lydia near the window he went back to the gateway to collect the ladder.

As his footsteps receded, Lydia was afraid. Alone, even though there were two people the other side of the stout walls more afraid than herself. The moonlight teased her with dancing shadows. Her back felt the chill of vulnerability, the trees held imaginary eyes, each movement was someone crouched, preparing to pounce. Every sound was a precursor of danger. She felt an atavistic desire to run.

Fortunately Matthew reappeared almost immediately, and she helped him to push the ladder up to drop it through the opening. He then sat on the window's edge guiding Tomos's attempts to secure the ladder and encouraging Molly to stay calm. Although by this time, Molly was treating the whole thing as a joke. Once the temporary prisoners were safely on the windowsill, the ladder was hauled through and reset to enable them to climb down onto the path.

Molly and Tomos carried the ladder and led the way back down to Stella's house which, Stella laughingly said, was becoming the first aid post for castle victims. More slowly, Matthew walked with Lydia, his arms around her, comforting her out of a fear she had long forgotten. His arms were so reassuring she thought she would never be afraid of anything again.

Although enjoying being a part of the adventure, Stella was worried about the couple's exploits. "I don't think you should go there again," she warned. "Whoever's up there could be dangerous."

"We don't know if anyone pushed those rocks over, Mrs Stevens," Tomos said. "The pathway wasn't made by castle builders, to last for centuries, just kids making an easy way in."

"But what if there is someone up there?" Lydia said. "It can't be coincidence: three times someone has tried to discourage people from going there. Dad didn't hit himself on the back of the head and I'm sure Gimlet didn't do it!"

"Probably a tramp," Molly said. "He'd be so pleased to find a place to spend the winter he'd want to keep it for himself."

"Luxury, that old castle, for someone without a home," Tomos agreed. He winked at Molly slyly and added, "Lying under the stars at night, earth for a pillow and the moon for a blanket."

"You're getting poetical, aren't you Tomos?" Lydia said, seeing the look of conspiracy that passed between the couple.

"You're probably right, it must be a tramp, some of them can be a bit unhinged," Stella agreed. "Poor man, let's hope he won't be disturbed any more."

"What are you doing back here?" Tomos asked Matthew who had been quiet during the conversation.

"Just a holiday. I plan to go walking in the Brecons before going back to take up a new post as headmaster in a school in Hereford."

"I'd never imagined you as a teacher," Tomos

laughed. "I bet if the parents knew some of the things you did as a kid, they'd have you sacked." He turned to Lydia. "Matthew Hiatt was the sort of boy all mothers warned their children against. Isn't that right, Matthew?"

"I can't deny it," Matthew laughed. "I was chased by the mothers, fathers, and even the police a few times. But things change, you grow up."

"But tearaway to school teacher, that's quite a jump," Stella said. "Good for you, Matthew. You've done well."

"It was Rosie's disappearance that changed me. With Mam and Dad too busy fighting each other to care what I did, there was only Rosie and when she left, I knew I had to move on." He turned to Lydia. "I lived with my grandmother for a while but she didn't really want me there, so I joined the army. It was there I began my education. Finished it when I was released and, well, that's my story."

"So you aren't back here for good?" Tomos asked.

Again Matthew looked at Lydia before replying. "No, not for good. More's the pity."

"Goodness, look at the time," Stella said, rising and beginning to gather the cups and saucers.

"I'll walk Lydia home," Matthew offered. "Perhaps I'll go in and make some excuses to her father."

"No need," Lydia smiled. "Mam and Dad will be asleep long since."

As they were leaving, Matthew looked at the bow window of Stella's house. "Wasn't this a hairdresser's once?" he asked. "Or has my memory failed me?

"It was, and you should remember. You kicked my cellar window in twice!" she said sharply. "I closed the business years ago. I didn't want to continue with it once Sam died." Stella didn't explain that it was looking after her sister Annie, and not the death of her husband, that had made it necessary to close down her very lucrative business.

"I'm glad my memory wasn't wrong," Matthew smiled. "Sorry, about the windows. Now, on Sunday we must all meet and you can show me around the place and introduce me to anyone who would remember me."

"As long as they haven't been saving a hiding for some remembered misbehaviour," Tomos laughed.

"Like smashing windows," Stella added severely.

Stella watched as the four people walked towards the main road. "Matthew Hiatt," she muttered. "I wonder what he really wants? Surely he isn't hoping to find his sister after all these years?"

Chapter Four

Glyn was working at The Pirate. Besides cleaning the cellars, he was employed to paint the walls in the kitchen and store room, which necessitated moving a huge number of boxes and containers. He was very tired, as, besides the work at the pub, he helped out with the taxi whenever Tomos or Gimlet needed a few hours off, and he had even found a few hours work digging over a garden or two.

"I don't know what's got into the boy," Billy said to Lydia one Sunday morning. "He told Gimlet and Tomos he wouldn't be working with them at Howe's Taxis, and there he is snatching every hour he can. He's acting as if money is the only thing that matters."

"This Cath of his must have grand ideas," Lydia replied, rubbing harder at the brass fender. "Perhaps she won't have him until he can buy her a house and all that goes with it. Some girls are like that, unwilling to start small and build a home together."

"I think he's in trouble," Billy said. "He's been in the navy since he was a boy and should have some savings, but he's grubbing about for every penny like he's got debts. Gimlet thinks it might be gambling. Why don't you try and persuade him to talk? If we knew the problem we might help."

"Not my place to interfere, Dad. He made it clear

that he and I were nothing more than friends. And I don't even know if I want that. Glyn isn't my responsibility, let this 'Cath' woman sort it out."

Since talking to Matthew Hiatt it was easier for Lydia to talk so casually about Glyn. Glyn had hurt her badly but Matthew, with his deep, fascinating eyes so filled with admiration for her, had eased the pain in a remarkable way. She remembered how safe she felt with him beside her walking up to investigate the cries from the castle, and the way he held her hand on their return when fear was no longer an excuse.

When there was a knock on the door at mid-morning, she opened it still flushed from polishing and dusting the living room. Expecting Molly, she felt flustered at seeing Matthew there, looking at her with a hesitant smile on his tanned face. "Am I disturbing you?" he asked.

"Of course not, come in," she smiled, patting her hair and hoping she didn't look a mess.

He stepped inside and followed her up to the living room.

"It's Matthew, Dad," she said unnecessarily.

"I called to see if you are all right after yesterday's adventure," he explained. With unconcealed admiration in his eyes he added, "I can see that you are." He turned to Billy and said gallantly, "You have a lovely daughter, Mr Jones. And I wondered if you'd allow me to take her out this afternoon."

"That depends where you think of going," Billy responded ungraciously. He was confused. This wasn't like the Matthew Hiatt he remembered, all polite and mannerly. Besides, young men didn't approach fathers for permission to take girls out, not these days they didn't.

"Dad!" Lydia protested.

68

But Matthew laughed. "I want to walk around the village, relive a few memories, that's all. I promise we'll be back in good time and I will look after her."

Feeling foolish at his pompous response to what was after all only politeness, Billy stood up and walked towards the stairs. "I think I can hear your Mam calling," he muttered as he disappeared.

"Doesn't like me, your dad," Matthew chuckled. "I'll have to see if I can change his mind."

Being locked in the castle was a good story but one which neither Lydia nor Molly could tell. The thought of the distress the news would give to Tomos's wife, Melanie, was sufficient to hold Lydia's tongue and they easily convinced Stella to do the same. Having Matthew with whom to discuss it was, therefore, a luxury and when they met for their first date, Lydia chatted to him about the mystery of Tomos and Molly being locked in and about the attack on her father.

Telling Matthew about her father and Gimlet's plan to frighten the couple had them laughing. Making light of her father's injury, the story was embellished and exaggerated and Matthew's deepset eyes glowed as he looked into hers, giving a wonderful feeling of belonging. Sharing an adventure, even one so innocuous, had started their friendship with a closeness they might otherwise have taken weeks to achieve.

The walk around the village, and up over the top of the hill from where they could look down over the whole of the bay and the mountains beyond, was perfect. It was one of those days when the sun had burned off every vestige of mist revealing the distant hills as clearly as the boats bobbing below. There was excitement in the air which was more like spring than the approach of winter.

Matthew talked mostly about his childhood and his frequent brushes with the law. He likened himself to the notorious Neville Nolan and assured her that although the boy was a nuisance, he was likely to grow up into a model citizen.

"Like you?" she queried.

"Oh no, not as perfect as I," he teased. The smile on his face softened to admiration and Lydia felt her mind drift away from the hill and its view and thoughts of Neville Nolan and his little gang of ruffians. All she could see was those fascinating eyes and that tempting mouth. Her mind filled with the wonder of this new sensation, and a belief in love at first sight.

He put an arm around her and they walked in silence back through what had become a hollow lane, with the ground indented into a curve by years of wear, and trees and bushes arching high above them. Then down the long shallow steps back to the seafront.

They met several time during the following week, and although Lydia extolled the wonders of his company to Molly, the relationship was not as perfect as she described. It didn't take more than a few dates for her to realise that, although they talked a lot, it was she who imparted information, and he who listened. Matthew chattered easily about when he was young, telling her things about her father she hadn't known, including that he had courted her Aunt Stella before marrying her sister Annie. But of the years since he had left the village she learned little. She learned no more about him than what she and her father had guessed when they first saw him standing on the foreshore. And most of that had been wrong.

"How long have you been teaching?" she asked on one occasion.

"Since I left the army," was the brief reply. "At least, after college."

"Have you ever done anything else?"

"Not much, I've had a half-year off to travel."

"Oh, really? Where have you been?"

"Here and there."

It was impossible to ask further questions when none were allowed to develop into conversation or discussion and she felt uneasy, there was a closed-in look on his face that made her feel guilty of prying. Then he would smile and look at her with those deep, hooded eyes and say, "Lydia, I want to talk about you. My life has been boring. At least it was, until I came here to kick about a few old memories, and found you."

He asked about her plans for the future and was surprised when she admitted she had none.

"I, well, Glyn and I always thought we'd marry and I saw no further than that. I thought I'd work on the market stall until the babies came then settle into being a housewife and mother. I'll always have to look after Mam, too. I've never thought any further than that."

"Is that enough for you? Don't you have anything burning inside, something you'd love to achieve?"

"I suppose my expectations are low, compared with yours, but I was content to work at the stall, earn a little extra with what I could make and—."

"You said, 'I *was* content'," he said, pouncing on the words. "Does that mean you're no longer content to accept what you presently have?"

"I haven't made any plans," she said hesitantly.

"For a start, why work for someone else?"

"What alternative is there?"

"Giving most of the profit for the things you make

71

to your boss seems like idiocy to me. Sell them yourself and get a bigger bite of the cherry."

"How can I do that?" she laughed. "Carry them around on my back and knock on doors looking for customers?"

"You wouldn't be the first to start that way. Besides, getting a shop isn't that impossible. What about that house where your aunt lives? That was a shop once, why not reopen that?"

"It was a hairdresser's."

"So?" He was staring at her so intently she began to feel uncomfortable. "Don't underrate yourself, Lydia."

"I couldn't," she said. "I'm not the type to run a business, learn something new." Thinking of Stella's shop she envisaged becoming a hairdresser and, knowing it wasn't what she wanted to do, his words were forgotten almost as soon as they were uttered. Besides, his lips, so close to her own, threw all serious thought out of the window. All her mind could grapple with was the kiss that hovered between them. The kiss when it came engulfed her. She felt herself drifting out of her depth, and fast.

Their need to see each other grew and Stella occasionally helped them to steal a few hours together by sitting with Annie for an hour while Billy went out for his usual couple of pints. On those occasions Billy didn't always go to The Pirate to meet his friends. Sometimes Lydia returned to find him sitting talking to Stella, sharing a pot of tea.

Matthew seemed very anxious not to annoy her father. "He remembers the old Matthew Hiatt and I have to prove to him that the wild boy has gone for ever."

Whenever they went out for the evening, she was

always brought home by ten o'clock. "He treats me like something fragile and precious," she confided in Molly. "So different from Glyn."

Each night after they parted she would lie awake, re-living their kisses and the way he looked into her eyes so her insides melted, and wondered at the magical way her life had been transformed since she had first spoken to him the night they had rescued Molly and Tomos from the castle. Sometimes, between the dreamlike repetitions of past meetings and dreams of the next date, she thought of Glyn and felt a tiny sensation of remorse and sadness that it was this fascinating stranger and not Glyn who was filling her mind and awakening her body.

Matthew enjoyed the cinema and was quite knowledgeable about its stars. They laughed through comedies and hugged each other through thrillers and after a couple of weeks Lydia began to wonder if Matthew would be the man with whom she would spend the rest of her life. Then he disappeared.

After a particularly happy evening during which he gave her a large box of expensive Lintz chocolates and a beautiful bouquet of roses and took her to dine at a rather splendid restaurant, they strolled home beside the sea. They stopped occasionally to kiss, their arms around each other in the privacy of the dark night. He told her she was beautiful and gentle and loving, all the things a true woman should be, then took out a small jeweller's box. Inside she found a silver bracelet, with three lucky charms on it; a dolphin, a mermaid and a seahorse.

"Matthew, thank you! It's beautiful!"

"So are you."

They delayed going home and instead walked along the front to the next beach. There, sitting on the rocks, with only the sound of the sea as accompaniment, he told her he loved her.

The next day he was gone.

It had begun to be a habit for him to walk with her to the bus as she set off for work and this morning he wasn't there.

"I bet he's overslept and is still peacefully sleeping," Lydia smiled as she and Molly found their seats.

"What were you doing to him last night then?" Molly teased and saw a flush of embarrassment flood her friend's face. "Serious, is it?" she whispered.

"I don't know. It might be," Lydia said hesitantly. "Too early to say. I know I like him, he makes me feel that life is good."

"But you still have regrets about Glyn?" Molly asked.

"No," Lydia replied. But the answer was not completely true. Although she and Matthew were happy together and laughed a lot, and he had told her he loved her, there was a residue of doubt. She knew he was holding something back, that he was not showing his true self. She smiled and added, "He mentioned taking me to a dance on Saturday. Dad's giving me the money to buy a new dress."

"Lucky old you. For my dates I have to put on my oldest clothes and heavy boots," Molly chuckled.

"You're still seeing Tomos then?"

"Not at the castle, mind!" She smiled secretly. "Found somewhere new we have and I'm not telling a soul where it is. We don't want any more frights like the last one."

Gimlet showed his unease whenever Matthew Hiatt was mentioned. "He bothers me," he told Billy one

74

evening when they were sitting in The Pirate. "You ought to know why."

"Because of Rosie, you mean?"

"Of course because of Rosie."

"It's all so long ago. Matthew is curious to see the place where he was born and spent the first sixteen years of his life, there's no chance he's going to stir up gossip. Not after all this time."

"I remember the day she left," Billy said. "I'd seen her the previous evening, remember? You and Mary were sitting with Annie and me pretending to go and visit old Henry Golding who was in hospital."

"I remember," Gimlet said. He was staring intently at Billy. "You had a row."

"She wanted me to leave Annie, and when I said I wouldn't she asked for money so she could go away and make a fresh start." Billy's eyes were sad as he brought the scene back to mind. "She told me she was pregnant, but I didn't believe her."

"You have no idea where she went?"

"None," Billy shrugged. "I did try and find out, mind, but she covered her tracks well. Didn't want to be found, that's my guess."

"You really haven't an idea?"

Billy looked curiously at Gimlet. "Of course I haven't! I'd have said, wouldn't I? Young Matthew was demented, searching for her. He was a troublesome child but I was sorry for him when she left. He didn't have anyone else, except that grandmother out in Bridgend. He went to live with her, I remember, but moved on as soon as he could arrange it, and joined the army. I didn't like the boy, but I'd have helped him find his sister if I'd known where she went." He looked at Gimlet who still looked unconvinced. "I'd have said!"

"Yes," Gimlet nodded. "You'd have said."

The Pirate was filling up and Glyn and Tomos pushed through the doors and struggled through the crowds to join them. Tomos ordered drinks and the brothers at once began arguing.

"I'm giving you all the work I can! I have to live too!" Tomos said. "It would be different if you'd come on a permenant basis as we'd planned, but now, well, you made your choice and you'll have to live with it. If you'd put all this money you're stashing away into the business instead of grabbing your wages like a junky after his fix, and putting it into some secret deal of your own we might sort something out."

"I don't have the money," Glyn insisted.

"What have you done with it? All those years at sea and now working for us and doing a few shifts at the pub cleaning the cellars, even stacking shelves in the shop after closing. You must be rolling in it boy. Living home with Mam and Dad and from what I hear giving as little as you can get away with, what are you doing with it. Salting it away for a world cruise?"

"I'm broke," Glyn said tightly, "that's all you need to know."

"Is that why you finished with our Lydia?" Billy asked.

"There's no Cath in London, I'm sure of that," Tomos said, banging the glasses onto the table and slopping some liquid. "Never no letters, and you haven't been to see her. So what is it, Glyn?"

"We talk on the phone," Glyn said.

"You don't use the one at home and you're too mean to phone London from a phone box!"

"*My* business! That's what it is!" Glyn stood up, pushing the table with the force of his anger. "My business. Right?"

"If you're living home with Mam and Dad it's their business too!" Tomos shouted back.

"If you're in trouble you know we'll help," Gimlet said more quietly. "Not gambling is it? Fools game gambling is, for sure."

"I'm just broke, that's all. Cath is – well, she'll wait for me." He looked at Billy and asked more calmly, "Is Lydia all right? I understand she's been seeing a lot of that Matthew Hiatt."

"What if she is?" Billy said with unaccustomed anger created by Tomos's concern. "What Lydia does is nothing to do with you remember! Let her down you did or she wouldn't have looked at anyone else and you know it!"

"I don't trust him," Glyn persisted. "He doesn't say why he's here and doesn't open up when people try to be friendly. Watch him, Billy, Lydia might be too trusting."

"You're right there," Billy said glaring at him. "She trusted you, didn't she?"

Glyn was worried about Lydia's obvious infatuation with Matthew and he waited for her when the stall closed on the following day and offered her a lift home. "I was in town dropping off a fare, so I thought I'd try and get here before you left," he explained.

"Yes, it will save me some time." She was glad of the lift but pride made her accept with only the minimum of thanks.

"Going out tonight?" he asked.

"Yes," she said. But she didn't explain that she was going to see her Auntie Stella and not meeting Matthew, which she knew was the reason for Glyn's question. She looked up at him, bright-eyed with defiance, and a feeling of guilt, foolish but real, invaded her with discomfort. She hadn't seen Matthew but was too unhappy about his disappearance to tell anyone, especially Glyn. "Matthew took me to dinner in the Chelsea Parlour last week." She forced a smile, refusing to show Glyn she was unhappy.

"That's expensive," he said.

"He can afford it and he thinks I'm worth it!" she snapped, wishing he would go away and not disturb her and spoil her mood. "He buys me flowers and expensive chocolates and treats me like I'm someone very special."

"You are," he said with a hesitant smile.

"He thinks so and can afford to show me," she replied.

"Lucky old him!"

She touched the bracelet she had worn every day since Matthew disappeared but didn't mention it. "Sorry, Glyn, I've got to go, I've got to get the meal ready for Mam and Dad and I have to be out by half-seven."

"Watch him, Lydia," Glyn warned. "Better still, stay right away from him. He's trouble that one, always was. I can feel it every time I look at him."

"Go away, Glyn!" she snapped. "Stay out of my life, it was where you chose to be, remember? Out of my life?" Hurriedly pushing him aside, she ran up the steps and into the house.

She was early, not having to wait for a bus and glad her parents were not yet home from Auntie Stella's. Tears ran down her rosy cheeks. Were they tears of anger at his impertinence? Or frustration? Or regret? She couldn't decide which. She only knew that with Glyn telling her to stay away from Matthew, and Matthew, for reasons of his own, deciding to stay away from her, it had made his absence more difficult to cope with. What was wrong with her that first Glyn then Matthew told her she was wonderful then dropped her like the proverbial hot brick?

Banging the saucepans about to express her annoyance for the tears which came too readily, she peeled the potatoes roughly and put them on to boil. It would have to be a fry-up: eggs, bacon and boring old potatoes, boiled then fried with some vegetables added. Mam hated it and Dad wasn't too keen but she lacked the enthusiasm to do more.

Slapping down the bacon and cracking the eggs so fiercely on the side of the pan the yolks broke, she suddenly stopped and asked herself, why was she angry? Was Matthew's absence of two days so devastating? He hadn't let her down on a date, left her standing waiting for him to turn up, feeling and looking foolish, had he? He'd just gone off about his own business for a day or two. She had no reason to doubt he'd be back. Or was it Glyn making her restless and filling her with inexplicable frustration? Did Glyn still mean that much to her?

She fingered the bracelet again. Had it been Matthew's parting gift, wrapped up in talk of loving to make her remember him?

More calmly she extravagantly threw away the unattractive eggs and over-cooked bacon and the half cooked potatoes. She decided on sausages instead. Sausage and mash wasn't exactly cordon bleu but her parents would prefer it to her first effort which showed her ill-temper so clearly. Glyn was no longer a part of her life, his wishes were not important. Suggesting she gave up Matthew was an impertinence. She mashed the potatoes with enthusiasm, achieving feathery splendour, and felt calmer by the time Tomos and Billy brought her mother home.

Matthew failed to appear again that evening although she sat there sewing until long after midnight in case he came. On the following day there was still no sign and Lydia allowed her imagination to build up her fears. She stopped pretending she knew where he was, and when he was returning, and told her father he had gone.

"What could have happened to him? He's vanished," she told her father. "Just like his sister did all those years ago."

"Don't be soft, girl," Billy said. "How could he? Besides, Rosie Hiatt didn't vanish like some conjurer's trick, she left the town."

"What happened to her, Dad?"

Billy shrugged. "No one knows for certain. I know the police were interested in Matthew, they had him in their sights for several petty crimes in the area, but Rosie . . ." he hesitated, about to explain about her summonses for prostitution, but decided that Lydia wouldn't be happier knowing, so instead he shrugged and said, "Rumours abounded. She was off to marry a wealthy man in England. She was joining the Salvation Army and repenting her wicked ways. She went to live on a Kibbutz. One story was that she went off with a band of Gypsies!"

"What wicked ways?"

"Oh, she was a bit of a flirt, that's all." He patted Lydia's hand. "Don't worry, love, if he's right for you he'll be back."

"Will he?" she asked Molly wistfully as the bus trundled along taking them home from work the following day. "I wish I could believe that."

* * *

80

The tall man was careful to enter the castle ground only when it was too late for anyone to be around, or when darkness and rain impeded the view. He had seen Stella once or twice, staring up at the ruin as if watching him, and he wondered superstitiously if the woman had second sight or had eyes that could penetrate the darkness, but decided she was just taking a breath of air before retiring. Although there was no possibility of her seeing him, let alone be able to identify him later, being such a distance away and in darkness, he still waited until he saw the light go on in her bedroom before shinning up the rope and dropping almost silently into the castle to begin his night's work.

On two occasions he had a narrow escape. A man with a dog on a lead, walked through the wood and up to the fence as he was about to climb over and enter the castle grounds. The dog growled and the owner stood for a moment, looking towards the tree where the tall man stood flexing his muscles and slowly raising the branch he held. Then the dog was distracted by a movement further away and dog and owner turned towards the quarry edge, and the tall man breathed out slowly between clenched teeth.

The second close encounter was with Gimlet. Puzzled, the tall man followed without a sound as Gimlet shinned over the gate and ran up towards the castle gates. He watched as Gimlet climbed the wall and went through the window, using a rope tied to an ash tree. Then he headed for the kitchen, studying the ground with the aid of a torch before snapping off the light and returning the way he had come.

The tall man smiled. The time he took replacing the turves so no one would see evidence of his digging had been well worth it, but what could the man have been looking for? An object lost while enjoying a bit of secret courting, perhaps? Maybe he was looking for the bicycle clips he had found on his first night of digging! he mused.

Putting aside concern for the man's motives he turned his mind to the night's work and began to lift out the first sod.

Billy had a bit of a cold that weekend and taking advantage of him staying at home with Annie and not going to clean out the allotment shed as he had planned, Lydia went to see her aunt. Dismayed at the unexplained absence of Matthew she didn't feel able to discuss it with Molly. Molly's attitude to boyfriends was so different from her own and, although Molly would undoubtedly laugh her out of her melancholy, she needed a serious discussion about her future and for that, Auntie Stella was her choice. Without bitterness, she knew her mother would put her own needs before reccommending any changes in her daughter's life.

Her knock was unanswered and she stood at the gate for a few moments undecided whether to wait or look at the shops and return later. The castle looked benign in the brightness of the winter sun and the ivy which clothed its walls was a brilliant green. The castle isn't the cause of the trouble, Lydia told herself, it was people who had created that. The thought comforted her. Perhaps she would even be brave enough to go there again if the need arose. Sadly she thought it would not be with Matthew holding her hand.

"Go on in, love, the door isn't locked." Stella appeared round the corner having walked along the road behind the shops. "Still looking up at that old castle and wondering what went on there, are you?"

"Sort of," Lydia smiled. "It doesn't look half so frightening during the day, does it?"

"I've lived here, under the shadow of its walls all my life," Stella said chuckling, "and I don't think it holds any terrors for me. When you take away the mysteries caused by courting couples who shouldn't be courting, and little boys playing out their own fantasies, you'll find there's little left that can't be explained!"

"I don't think Molly will go there again," Lydia said.

"Perhaps not Molly, but someone is for sure. I've seen someone moving up there and once, very late at night a man came past my gate, stood in the shadow of my wall for about twenty minutes. I thought it was Gimlet, but then he hopped over the gate as nimble as a hurdler so I decided it couldn't have been him! Taller too, more like that Matthew Hiatt only bigger in build. Seen anything of him lately?" she chattered on while unpacking her shopping. "Nice looking he is, mind, but as big a mystery as what went on at the castle, don't you think?"

"I haven't seen him for days," Lydia blurted out sadly. "He's gone, Auntie Stella. And he didn't even say goodbye. We were getting on so well and we'd half arranged to go to a dance last Saturday but he never called and I haven't seen him since." She thought of the wonderful and extravagant evening at The Chelsea Parlour and told her aunt that she realised now that it had been a goodbye.

"You've been to his lodgings?"

"He paid his bill and left on the morning after we last met."

Over a cup of tea and some home-made cake, Lydia talked. She poured out all her hurt and Stella listened in silence. Then Stella stood up, brushed the crumbs from her lap into the grate and said firmly, "You, my girl, have to plan your future. Drifting along waiting to marry is all right while you have a partner with the same idea but now you're on your own and you must make the most of it." Being one of those people unable to sit with idle hands, Stella reached for the child's cardigan she was knitting. As they discussed alternatives for Lydia to consider, she suddenly held up the garment and said, "Why don't you leave that stall and work for yourself?"

"Matthew suggested the same thing!" Lydia stared at her aunt, her face open with surprise, then her expression faded and she said the same to Stella she had said to Matthew. "How can I?"

"Easy. Open up the shop here," Stella replied, unknowingly again making the same suggestion as Matthew.

"I don't know anything about running a business like that."

"How d'you know before you've given it a try?" Stella repeated Matthew's words again.

"How can I?" This was a day for echoes she thought with slight irritation. "What do I know about hairdressing?"

"Hairdressing? Who said anything about hairdressing? I mean to sell wool and hand-knitted garments. Some factory-mades too, to bring more trade. It isn't a bad spot here, right opposite the castle where visitors pass in the summer."

This was something different. This was worth considering.

"But, don't you need a lot of money to open a shop?"

"Not if we're careful. We'd have to start small,

mind. Tell you what, I'll keep this little cardigan," she waved her knitting with enthusiasm, "and the others I've made ready to take for your Mrs Thomas, and instead, they'll go to start the stock-pile for 'Lydia Jones, Quality Knitwear and Wool', how will that be?"

Two hours later, Lydia left her aunt's house buoyed up with excitement and with plans and ideas buzzing through her head. With Stella promising her six months before she charged her rent, and also agreeing to help run the place while looking after Annie, it seemed so right, that Lydia had already decided to do it before she reached home.

She burst in through the door, climbing the stairs from the kitchen calling to her parents, "Mam, Dad, I'm going to open a shop, what d'you think of . . ." her words petered out as she saw Glyn standing beside the window looking out of the window. "Hello, Glyn," she managed, before going into her room to take off her coat.

She stood in her bedroom, angry that he was here, just when she needed to discuss what she and Auntie Stella had decided. Now she would have his opinions and interruptions and no doubt her mother would seek his support, try to discourage her, and was probably already telling him how impossible it all was.

Childishly she was tempted to wait in her room until she heard him going downstairs and out of the house. Instead, she touched up her make-up and combed her hair and went back into the living room looking, if not feeling, confident and controlled. I'm a businesswoman, or almost, she told herself. Glyn's opinion isn't relevant. Her spurious confidence took its first dive as she reminded herself it was her mother, not Glyn, whom she had to convince.

"I can't see how we'll manage," was Annie's predictable first comment. "Stella won't have time for you to be under her feet all fuss and feathers. Selfish of you to think of it," she added.

"It was Auntie Stella's idea. Hers, and Matthew's!" she added looking defiantly at Glyn. "He thinks I'm foolish to go on working for someone else, giving away a large chunk of my profits. Knitting and getting the full price makes better sense, he said."

"There's rent and light and heating and—" Glyn began hesitantly.

"All considered and thought of. Auntie Stella is going to invest in me by letting me have the shop free for a few months," Lydia retorted sharply. "You don't honestly think I'd consider starting a business and not be aware of those basic needs do you?"

"I think it's a wonderful idea," Billy said. "And very kind of Stella to offer her help. Fancy, my daughter a business woman!"

"What about me?" Annie sounded genuinely frightened and Lydia hastily reassured her.

"You'll be with Auntie Stella, and I'll be there as well. There won't be any difference so far as you're concerned, I promise, Mam."

"If Tomos and I can help," Glyn said, "we'll be happy to run you to wholesalers and the like."

She ignored Glyn, pretended she hadn't heard, didn't want to say thank you, didn't want him involved. He'd let her down once and she wasn't giving him the chance to do so again. It was impossible for her to smile and to thank him. She turned to her father. "I'll make a list of the firms who supply the stall, that isn't cheating, is it, Dad? Then I'll give my notice next Friday. I'll be free to start working for myself before Christmas with any luck."

When Glyn shrugged himself into his coat and prepared to leave, Billy insisted he stayed for a cup of tea. "Lydia's made some pasties for tea, stay and have one, she always makes plenty."

So Lydia had to go down and prepare food for them when all she wanted to do was think about this new project. Having Glyn silently watching her was taking the joy out of it, part of her wished she could involve him and wild thoughts danced in her head, remembering how easily they had once shared every thought, every plan.

That route swiftly led her to the memory of hearing he was leaving her for someone else. Sentimental dreams of even friendship being restored were snapped off sharply. There was no love and no prospect of friendship. Now, when she thought of loving, it was the dark-eyed Matthew who filled her mind and had her body racing with the prospect of fulfillment. Yet the memories of when she and Glyn were together refused to fade away.

Glyn followed her down the stairs to the kitchen and watched as she put the pasties in the oven to warm. He set the tray with plates and cups and saucers as he had many times before. Her thoughts continued to play tricks, one minute thinking this was how it had always been, then being brought up sharp to memories of him telling her goodbye. She was very conscious of him as he whistled cheerfully and helped load the second tray, putting out napkins and finding the cutlery with the ease of regular practice.

"How is – Cath?" she asked, hiding her expression as she bent over the oven.

"Cath is fine. She and I are still searching for a flat," he said.

"London, is it?"

"Probably, yes."

"Good-looking is she, this Cath?"

"Well, yes, I suppose she is."

"His answers were curt, he obviously didn't want to discuss his new lady-love with me," Lydia told Molly the following morning on their way to work.

"More fool you for trying!" Molly said unsympathetically. "I'd have told him to drop dead if he even spoke to me after what he did to you!"

"D'you know, Molly, I know this sounds silly, but I don't think there is a 'Cath in London'. I think he's made her up."

"Tomos thinks so too," Molly said. "He thinks he's got a girl pregnant and has to pay her maintenance every week and that's why he's broke."

For some reason Lydia found this easier to bear than the thought that he had found someone else he loved more than her. A moment's weakness and then regret she could now understand. After all, wasn't that what had happened to Glyn's brother? But if it were true, she would never marry him. Not when someone else had more right to him, a stronger need of him. For the first time she began to wonder if there was someone else in Matthew's life. Perhaps he had a wife somewhere, a man didn't necessarily wear a wedding ring, so it was easy to be deceived. "Do you think Matthew is married or has a fiancée somewhere?" she asked her friend.

"What if he has? A brief bit of fun wouldn't harm her, she'd never find out, would she?"

Lydia was silent for a while. That wasn't the way she looked at things. A relationship had to be true and honest or she would prefer not to have one at all. Best she forget both Matthew and Glyn and concentrate on the business she and her aunt were planning. In a low voice she began explaining to Molly what she was going to do. For a while anyway, it would keep her busy and with little time to think about the undependable Glyn, or the mysterious Matthew Hiatt.

Chapter Five

The setting up of the business took a lot of Lydia's time. She constantly sneaked off from the market to telephone to one department after another and saw various accountants and tax officers until she began to think it would have been simpler to continue working on the market stall and selling what she made to friends.

"It's never-ending," she complained to Stella one Sunday morning two weeks later. "It's like working my way through a jungle and never finding the way out. Every time I think I've got there, the path opens out into three more and I don't think I'll ever come to the end of it."

They were giving the shop an intermediate clean, as half the room had already been fitted out with shelves and display areas. The bow window shone with Stella's efforts and the new shelves were being covered with attractive paper awaiting the arrival of their stock of wool. Boxes of jumpers and children's clothes were stacked both in the shop and in Stella's living room. From the cellar they had unearthed a pair of stools and a glass-fronted display cabinet in which they planned to show some of their better quality knitwear. Knitting with sequins was one of Stella's specialities.

"I think I'll end up living in the shed out the

back if he doesn't finish the shelves soon," she sighed.

"Who's doing the work, you haven't said?" Lydia queried.

"Well, if you must know, it's Glyn. Now—" she held out a hand to stop Lydia's protest. "I know you said you didn't want him to help but he offered and, he's doing it for nothing, so you needn't go on about him grabbing all the money he can. Only costing us the price of the wood it is, and if there'd been a storm I think he'd have used driftwood to save us even that, so careful he's being. Now, we have to be grateful, don't we? A shoe-string operation this is after all."

"I understand and I don't blame you, but I don't want to be grateful to Glyn."

"No fuss, I'll thank him for the pair of us! Now, I'll make the tea while you finish putting paper on that last shelf. Coming in to do the ones on this side tomorrow he is."

"Then I'll stay away!"

"Best for you too. I don't want him distracted and putting them vertical instead of horizontal," Stella quipped.

"Has he said anything about this new girlfriend, er . . ." she put her head on one side quizzically, "Cath is she called?"

"You know very well she's called Cath and no, he hasn't discussed her. I have the feeling he's regretting telling you goodbye and wants a chance to put things right."

"Pity for him! I won't be messed about again!"

"I can understand your anger, *fach*, but don't let pride keep you from being happy. It's no fun watching your life slip away watching the man you should have married instead of being with him."

Something in her aunt's voice made Lydia turn and stare. "Auntie Stella? You don't mean you were unhappy with Uncle Sam?"

"No love, not unhappy. He was a good, kind man, but there was someone else and I turned him away. It's a constant regret, not forgiving him then for something that seems so trivial now."

It was late when Lydia left the house near the castle gate and she automatically glanced up at the dark walls. It was Stella who heard the howling first, and she looked up and frowned. "Whatever's that?"

"Sounds like a dog. Could it be lost?" Lydia was at once sympathetic and wanting to help. "It isn't far from the gate, perhaps if I climbed over and offered it some food I'd be able to catch it?"

A piece of meat from the Sunday roast was found and Lydia carefully climbed over the gate and dropped down into the darkness of the grounds. The dog heard her and ran to her, but then as she leaned forward to offer the morsel, and her shadow loomed before her like a dark cloak, it ran back up towards the high walls of the ruin. Lydia was handed a torch and without putting it on, she followed.

She found the dog, a young, smooth-haired terrier, shivering against the wall near the tall castle gates, and this time it allowed her near enough to pick it up and begin to carry it down the slope to the gate. Half way down it became agitated and struggled to get free. It managed to jump from her arms and Lydia gasped in frustration as it ran once again up to the wrought-iron gates.

Inside the castle the tall man was digging out his first spadeful of the night. He was puzzled. Surely he should have come upon it before this? He frowned, and looked around him at the remnants of the kitchen walls, then he paced out the area he had already examined and decided that, as time was beginning to run out, he would move and start again against the furthest wall. He cursed silently, angry with himself for the haziness of his memory. He had expected it to be so easy.

He heard the dog whining and was irritated. He didn't want anything untoward happening to bring people sniffing around. If the stupid animal had been inside the castle he would have aimed a blow at it and made it run, but separated by the thick walls, it was out of his reach and he could only hope it would soon get fed up and go back where it belonged.

He dug out three sods in the new area, wondering if he was doing the right thing, glancing back to the place he had reached the night before. Perhaps he should have continued in his methodical way, not start losing his nerve digging in panic, running around chasing his own tail.

He was concentrating, still undecided on where to dig, when the dog began howling. Low at first, increasing in pitch and volume, ululating, unearthly, filling the air and echoing around the ancient stones. In spite of his cold determination to find what he had come for he paused momentarily, fighting off that age-old survival instinct; the urge to run. It was such an eerie sound, tragic and despairing.

It was as the howling increased in intensity with the dog raising his head to the sky and issuing a wavering soprano, that he felt his spade touch something. At last! Shading the torch with a hand he knelt down beside the disturbed turf and reached out to scrabble around in the loose soil.

Against the walls the dog continued to howl, the

sound of it entering his head, giving actual pain with the piercing quality of the note. He forced himself to concentrate on his find, hoping it was the object for which he had been searching.

At first he thought he had found a necklace of large white beads then he gave a low growl of horror and fell back onto the grass. It was a hand. A skeletal hand.

Holding a hand to his mouth as sickness threatened, he backed away then turned and ran to where he had entered. His back felt unbelievably chilled, as if it were illuminated in ice ready for an assailant to use as a target. Scrambling, uncaring about being seen, he almost fell out of the ruin and staggered drunkenly down the slope.

As Lydia picked up the dog again, she heard the noise of someone or something crashing through the bushes and she gripped the dog tightly as it struggled to escape from her. For the second time she couldn't hold it and it jumped from her arms and ran to the wall and pressed its small body against the stones, shivering in terror. Wanting to run but determinedly brave, she ran back towards the crashing sounds, intending to grab the dog before making her escape from whatever was about to appear.

The shadow bursting out of the trees was not unexpected, yet when it happened it was terrifying. She had almost arrived at the place where the dog sat shivering, still pressed against the stone wall, aware that whatever it was had almost reached her. The sounds increased in volume, the trees and bushes began to sway and then the apparition was upon her, huge, looming up suddenly out of the darkness and pushing her aside before running around, past the castle gates and down the slope in the direction of the sea.

Lydia was disorientated by the man's appearance and the push he had given as he passed that had swung her round. Staggering, she fell into the undergrowth her feet slipping on the steep slope. Down and down she slithered, her arms reaching out to grasp something to slow her fall, branches tearing cruelly at her skin. When she came to a stop she lay there afraid to move and it was a while before she could pull herself up. She saw that she had landed at the exact spot where Molly had fallen.

Defying her fears, convinced that the terrifying apparition was up there waiting for her, imagining she could hear his breathing, she climbed painfully up to where the dog now lay, staring wildly into the darkness. She picked it up and listened. There wasn't a sound. Slowly she walked to the castle entrance and stood, staring through the darkness towards the castle mound and the distant sea, but everywhere was silent. The man, whoever he was, had been swallowed up in the darkness leaving a silence that was more frightening than the crashing of his footsteps through the bushes as he ran towards her.

Lydia forced herself to stay calm, soothing herself by soothing the dog, and walked quickly but without running, down the slope to the gate where her aunt was anxiously waiting.

"What happened, *fach*? I thought I saw somone running away."

"There was a man and he pushed me down the slope," Lydia began.

"Not hurt are you?"

"No, just scratched. I don't think he was trying to frighten me away. I don't think I was in danger, big as he was. It was he who was frightened. He was running blindly, escaping from something that had terrified him." She handed the shivering animal to her aunt and said slowly, "Auntie Stella, I think I should go and see what it was that frightened him. I'm sure it wasn't the dog howling, or me wandering up there."

They jumped as footsteps came around the corner and for a moment they froze, Stella hugging the still trembling dog, wanting to run, but unable to move.

"What are you two doing out this time of night?"

The two women looked at each other and sighed with relief. It was Glyn's voice.

"Thank goodness you've come, *bach*," Stella said, "Lydia is talking of going up to the castle, now, this minute, mind. Looking to see what frightened that man into knocking her over."

The disjointed explanations were begun again and, when he understood Lydia's determination to go, Glyn willingly agreed to go with her. "But I wish you'd let me go alone," he pleaded. "You two stand here and I'll whistle to let you know I'm all right."

"No, Glyn. I'm going in. There's something going on up there and I want to see what it is."

"Not Molly and our Tomos this time then?"

"A man it was. Big, and running away from something he'd seen."

"Or done!" Glyn warned. "You can't take chances, Lydia. Heaven alone knows what had frightened him."

"I'm going to look," Lydia insisted.

Stella found a second torch and Glyn and Lydia set off up the slope and, finding the man's rope still hanging up and in through the window, climbed inside. The torches, creating strange shapes and making the walls appear to move, added to Lydia's fear, but she refused to show Glyn how afraid she was.

She walked a distance away from him, shining her torch on the grassy ground, briefly penetrating the darkness of the silent rooms, hardly looking and certainly not pausing to identify anything the beam revealed. She was so scared she wouldn't have recognised a group of terrorists armed with machetes and machine guns if the wavering light had revealed them.

"Come over here," Glyn whispered.

"I'm all right," Lydia said defiantly.

"Come with me," Glyn insisted. "We ought to stay together."

She walked to where he was waiting at the entrance to a barrel-vaulted store room, and he took her hand. A cursory look into the store room with its grille-enforced window, then they walked through the open corridor towards the entrance, where once guards had stood and forbade entrance to all but chosen visitors. In front of them, a little to the right of the entrance were the irregular remains of the kitchen walls.

Looking through the broken stonework, Glyn's torch beam exposed the disturbed earth and slowly, and with some trepidation, they moved closer to investigate. Although the room was open to the sky, and only a partial shell of what had once been the large kitchen with its three fireplaces, Lydia felt something close to claustrophobia as they stepped through the entrance. She could have jumped the lower areas of the walls with ease, yet it was like walking into a trap. She knew that if Glyn had not been with her she would not have had the nerve to do more than approach that doorway and wave her torch about.

Like the man who had been digging, they did not comprehend at first. Neither could ever have imagined finding a body, and their minds refused to accept that this was what they were looking at. For seconds neither spoke.

"It has to be a joke," Glyn whispered hoarsely. He reached out to hold her. "But I don't think it is."

Lydia instinctively moved closer to him, pressing herself against him, grateful for the warmth of his body close to her own. "Glyn, who can it be?"

"We have to get back and phone the police. It's up to them to find out."

Without words of intent between them they both knelt on the damp ground and offered a prayer for the dead person that he might find peace at last, now his secret death was known.

Slowly, no longer afraid, they turned to leave. Lydia's torch swung around the scene, wondering about the person whose life had ended in such an unlikely spot. That it had been a tragic end was certain, but whether the truth would be revealed was doubtful. She didn't know how long it took for a body to reach the state of this one, but guessed that it must be many years.

Some need for respect forbade her looking again at the body. Yet she no longer had the sensation of menace. With the disturbed turf and the small piles of earth surrounding the partially open grave, it was no longer a place of danger and shadows, fear no longer crackled in the air. The place was filled with poignancy, and sadness.

A spade had fallen to the ground and beside it a garden fork, its tines still sticky with soil, and near its handle, as if fallen from it, was a man's knitted hat. The torchlight reflected a pom-pom, green and unaccountably gay in the gradually weakening beam. Still in shock, and again hardly aware of what she was looking at, Lydia swung the beam back to the direction they would take and, with Glyn's hand in hers, returned to where her aunt and the now calm dog were waiting.

When Stella was told of their discovery, she wept. "Poor, poor man, all alone up there and with no one to mourn him," she sobbed. She put the dog down to hug her niece, and it at once scuttled through a hole in a hedge and ran up the path and disappeared. "It wasn't lost at all," Stella said in amazement, "he was just making sure that poor man was found."

Once the police were called, the night passed in complete confusion. Questions bombarded them, none of which had answers, and it was dawn before Lydia wearily made her way home.

Telling her parents was somehow less exciting that she might have imagined. She had intruded on someone's life and death and it was not a story to enjoy or make into some sensational news. Telling Molly was even less so.

"I feel so sad, that lonely dark place hiding such a tragedy. And only a few weeks ago, before the castle was closed for repairs, people were wandering around, peering and prying into all the corners, joking, laughing, admiring the magnificent views, while all the time that poor man lay undiscovered and unrevenged."

"Perhaps whoever killed him had returned, but why? What could he be wanting to dig him up for?" Molly queried.

"It didn't look like that to me. I think someone was searching for something else and just happened upon the body and made a run for it."

"That man, the one running from the castle and who knocked you into the bushes, any idea who it was?"

"None. It happened too quickly. There was a rush of sound as he pushed through the trees, running along the path, then he was on me, in such urgency to pass, grappling, knocking me over in his haste to get away."

"You're sure it was no one you recognised?"

"How could I? I was bending down trying to catch the dog."

"Doesn't it strike you as a strange coincidence that Glyn was there so quick?"

"Out for a walk he was."

"Often goes for walks at night, does he? Past your auntie's house? Nothing down there but a lane leading to the quarry."

"Molly! You aren't suggesting it was Glyn who was digging up there, are you? He was just as shocked as I was when we found it."

"He didn't lead you to it then?"

"No, of course he didn't!" Lydia said firmly. "We found it together." But doubts crept in as she relived the scene: her wandering off and Glyn calling, insisting they stayed together, waiting for her before walking through the open corridor past the storerooms and down towards the kitchen block. Could it have been he? "Of course it wasn't Glyn!" she repeated vehemently. But whether she was trying to convince Molly or herself she was no longer sure.

All that day and several following, the police were to be seen going to and from the castle. The high gates at the entrance had been opened and crowds gathered around the gate leading into the grounds, opposite Stella's house. The police were digging up

100

the whole of the kitchen floor in the hope of finding further clues to the tragedy. Lydia learned from the newspaper reports, that all they found was an old oiled jacket and a box containing money and a few oddments of jewellery which, it transpired, were part of the haul from a series of robberies committed several years before.

Two days after the body was discovered it was identified as that of Rosie Hiatt, Matthew's sister. By a coincidence, Lydia had a letter from Matthew that same day. He was walking in the Brecon Beacons, the letter posted in Brecon itself. The date written on the letter was the day before the body was found and it began with apologies.

'Dear Lydia,
Please forgive me for going off so suddenly, but I had an appointment to see someone and, well, the weather was so mild and winter seemed postponed so I couldn't resist spending a few days up here. I'll be back on Thursday and will call then to make my apology a personal one. I'll book for us to eat at the Chelsea Parlour, shall I?
Please forgive my rudeness and be ready for me when I call at seven-thirty on Thursday.'

He had signed it,

'affectionately yours,

Matthew.'

"How will I tell him?" she said to Molly. "How can you break such news gently?"

"What makes you think you'll have to tell him?" Molly queried. "That's for the police to do surely? They'll want to see his reaction for sure."

"Molly! You aren't saying he killed his own sister? First it's Glyn, now its Matthew. What about me? I was only five at the time, mind, so I'd have had a job to hit her over the head."

"Was that how she died? Being hit over the head?"

Lydia shrugged. "The police haven't said."

Molly was right and when Lydia showed Matthew's letter to the police they arranged to see him first and break the terrible news. "If by any chance you do see him before we find him," Detective Superintendent Richards said, "please don't tell him anything. Just tell him the police want to see him."

The Detective Superintendent stayed and talked to Lydia for some time, "I'm trying to help you get the horror of it out of your mind by discussing it fully," he explained kindly. "Tell me everything you remember about that night, who you saw, what you remember about the man." He touched her hand reassuringly. "It's best, believe me. If you can clear your mind of any details that might return and force you to relive the scene, you will soon be free of it."

He came again later the same day and admitted he was off duty but anxious to help her.

"Is there anything you can talk about regarding the days before the discovery of Rosie Hiatt's body? Did you see anyone hanging around the castle? Hear anything?"

Lydia shook her head. She hadn't mentioned Molly's thoughts on the convenient arrival of Glyn, although Richards mentioned that himself.

"I think I'd have known if Glyn had been digging

at the castle. The smell of disturbed earth is quite strong. It would have been on his clothes, like when my father has been working on the allotments," she explained.

"An allotment? Perhaps he saw something up there," the policeman frowned. "I think I'd better have another word. Now don't forget," he said as he stood to leave. "If you think of anything further that you haven't told us, call me, Detective Superindendent Richards, speak to me personally, that way you won't have to keep repeating everything to half a dozen people, right?" He patted her shoulder. "Now don't worry about it. Happened many years ago it did. Rosie Hiatt was a prostitute, did you know? Attract violence some of them, easy to choose the wrong client it is."

Lydia's thoughts went out to Matthew. Surely he wasn't aware of his sister's reputation? With this revelation, the discovery of her body, probably murdered, would be a double blow.

When Matthew alighted from the bus near the sea, the wind was blowing the tops off the waves, scattering litter along the streets and making people rush for cover. The sky was full of small clouds that hurried along bustled impatiently by a fierce wind. On the horizon, darker clouds threatened rain. He went to the hotel where he had phoned to retain a room, and when he asked for his key, the landlady said he should go first to the police station.

"What for?" Matthew smiled.

"I don't know, I was just told to tell you to go straight there as soon as you arrived."

"A cup of tea first?" he pleaded.

"Best you go straight away," she smiled sadly. "They'll get you a cup of tea up there for sure."

Matthew frowned, but leaving his rucksack near the desk he went to the police station, where he was interviewed by Richards.

Two other policemen were present and, after a few questions about his whereabouts during the past days, they told him that a body had been found which they believed to be that of his sister, Rosie.

"Rosie? My sister, Rosie? But she went off with someone, how could it be her? Where was she found? What happened to her?" he asked, as he stared white-faced at the policeman. He collapsed into a chair and covered his face with his hands. "Rosie? It can't be. There has to be a mistake." He looked up, his face ashen. "She disappeared and with no news of where she went. Where has she been living?"

"We have reason to believe she never left, sir. It seems likely she died at the time she disappeared. Your sister didn't go anywhere I'm afraid."

"But if she had an accident, why wasn't she found until now?" Matthew was shocked and his hands and forearms shook as he took the cup of tea they provided.

The policemen looked at each other. His reaction was no act. News of his sister's death had been a complete surprise and his grief too seemed genuine.

"Your sister's body was found buried inside the ruined castle."

"What?" There was pain in Matthew's eyes as he stared up at the superintendent.

"Someone appeared to be trying to dig up her remains, but we think he was disturbed, possibly by a dog howling outside. Anyway for whatever reason, he ran away and it was two people who went to investigate who made the sad discovery."

As realisation that she had been murdered dawned, Matthew was filled with grief. "Murdered? But – what happened?" he wanted to know, asking the question over and over as the policemen pressed him about things that seemed to him, irrelevant.

"We aren't certain what happened to cause her death. That will take a few more days," he was told. "But there's no way she could have buried herself, so we are naturally suspecting foul play. Your sister's death was probably murder."

"Who found her?" he asked. "The two people, who were they?"

"A young lady called Lydia Jones and Glyn Howe. Do you know them?"

"How awful for her. Yes, I know her." His agitation grew. "How terrible that she should come across – I have a date with her tonight, although I don't think I'll keep it now."

"Perhaps you should, sir. A pretty girl, a nice meal, not a bad way to overcome the shock?"

"She knows, does she, that the . . . that it was my sister?"

"She knows, sir."

"This isn't real," Matthew muttered.

"What do you mean, sir?"

"I mean murder is something in books, or on the films. It isn't something that happens to you."

"Sadly, sir, we know all too well how real it can be. Now, would you like to see a doctor? This has been a terrible shock to you, although I don't suppose you remember your sister very well, do you?"

"I remember she was only eighteen when she disappeared and that's too young to die!"

They coaxed him gently to make him talk about her, the sister he had said goodbye to when he was only seventeen, but his memories were sketchy and he was too shocked to think clearly.

"I know she wasn't popular with the women, too pretty she was, and too well liked by young husbands." He smiled then, a wavering smile. "I remember seeing her shouting back at a neighbour who was accusing Rosie of trying to steal her husband. Never had any need to steal, they came flocking, from what I remember."

The policemen were silent, they had on record that Rosie Hiatt was a prostitute, with several court appearances for soliciting. Seeing her brother, so grief-stricken to hear of her death, they thought his romantic version of the truth was best left intact. This wasn't the time for disillusion, the enquiry would reveal all that soon enough.

"How did you get back from Brecon, sir?" one of them asked.

"By bus."

"Oh, that's strange, we had men waiting at the railway station and watching the coaches. Do you happen to have saved your ticket, sir?"

"Why?"

The policeman shrugged and after searching through his pockets, Matthew gave them the crumpled bus ticket.

"We would appreciate the names and addresses of places you stayed, too."

Matthew shook his head. His deep-set eyes were filled with pain. "I only stayed with someone on the last night. I have a small tent and I've been using that."

"We tried to intercept you, sir. As I explained we

had men waiting at the coach station and the railway station in town. We didn't want you to find out about Rosie by seeing newspapers or the like."

"I did see the account of the find in the newspapers, but I never dreamt for one moment that it concerned me. Poor Rosie." He broke down then, shivering with the horror of it and was left, with yet another cup of tea until he felt able to leave.

"Just before you go, sir," Richards smiled and led him back to his seat. "We found something else at the castle."

"Something belonging to poor Rosie?" Matthew frowned.

"No, I don't think this was anything to do with Rosie. Unless her death was due to her finding out something she shouldn't. No, this wasn't Rosie's cup of tea at all. More yours!" The man's voice hardened and he stared at Matthew. "A bit wild you were when you were a young lad, weren't you?"

"What was it?"

"An old oilskin jacket which we think might have been wrapped around a gun."

"Was she – was my sister shot?"

"We can't reveal the cause of death at present, sir." The superintendent paused, then added, "There was something else found. A box containing a few items that were stolen in a spate of robberies about the time your sister disappeared, sir. We haven't recovered all the items stolen, just some of them."

"You think Rosie was involved in robberies?"

"We think they've been there as long as your sister's body. Her death and the robberies might be connected. She might have interrupted the thieves."

Matthew seemed dazed. He didn't appear to hear what was being said. "Can I go now?" he asked.

"Of course, but you won't be leaving the area, will you?"

"I have a new post, a Head Teachership, which starts after the Easter holiday. Will all this be cleared up by then?"

"By Easter? God 'elp, we hope so, sir."

Matthew didn't go back to his hotel, but walked to Lydia's home. It was a little early for her to be back from work but he would wait. He was choked with the emotional shock of knowing that a member of his family, his sister, had been killed, murdered. It was the strangest feeling, waves of disbelief and the hope there had been a mistake, followed by anger against the unknown person who had committed the ultimate crime and taken her life. He felt self-pity too, for the loss of the young girl he remembered as saucy, amusing, affectionate and pretty.

When Lydia turned to walk up the steps she was singing. A cheerful song that was making her smile. Then she saw him and stopped, laughter fading as she looked at his face; pale, thinner than she remembered, the eyes huge and filled with an agony she could only imagine. The eyes told her he knew.

"Oh Matthew, I'm so sorry," she said.

He was angry with himself for not controlling the sobs then which racked his body.

They went inside and mercifully Annie was not yet home, so they had a few minutes alone. He questioned her about how she and Glyn had found the body, what they were doing there, going over what she told him, sifting out and analysing every miniscule piece of information, needing to know even her deepest thoughts as she had looked down on his sister's remains. He was touched and reduced to tears when she told him how she and Glyn had prayed.

"I don't think we should go on our date after all," he said taking deep breaths to hold his voice steady. "I want to walk and walk, on my own, do you understand?"

"I'll be here all evening if you want to talk about it," Lydia said, but although she stayed up until past eleven, he didn't come.

When the police made Lydia go through the discovery of the body again, one of them remarked on the fact that there had been no digging tool found. They coaxed her to relive the moment when the body was seen, talking her through it slowly and methodically. "I remember I moved the torch beam around the area. I don't know why, I wanted to take my mind off the sight of that grave I think, looking at the ordinary to block out the extra-ordinary. I remember the uneven mounds of earth and the dreadful scar that was the grave and—"

"And?" the policeman coaxed.

"I remember seeing the fork and spade. They were thrown on the ground, and the fork had dirt on it, so it had been used."

"Good," the policeman encouraged. "Now, keep remembering, what else did you see? Think of yourself looking along the torch beam. Now, it's moving across the grass, seeing the grave and the tools, and . . .? What else did you see?"

Although she searched her mind diligently, she remembered nothing more.

Matthew met her as she closed the stall the following day and they walked to the bus station together.

"Have the police questioned you again?" Matthew asked. "I was there for two hours this morning, although I can't see how I could help. Too much time has passed."

"I did remember something more," Lydia told him. "They took me through that evening step by step. I remembered something I hadn't thought of when they talked to me before. They mentioned that no digging tools were found and I knew there was a fork and a spade when Glyn and I left the castle to call the police," she told him. "They're clever mind, making me see it all again. It was as if I wasn't really there, but just looking in on a scene in which others played the parts." She shivered at the memory. "Oh Matthew I can't help thinking that there must have been two of them. One man must have still been there, watching us, waiting for us to go so he could take the tools before making his escape."

"But you don't remember seeing anything else?" Matthew asked.

"No, I've remembered everything I'm going to," she said. "Now I want to put it out of my mind, at least until the inquest."

"I think you should. Forget it and try to think of something more cheering. Now, where shall we go tonight? Pictures?"

"As long as it's a comedy!" she replied.

They didn't stay in the cinema very long. Lydia could see Matthew's mind wasn't on the film, he was staring down at his hands, or fidgeting in his seat.

"Come on, Matthew, let's go home," she said and he willingly agreed.

The living room was full when they arrived at the house overlooking the bay. Billy was looking very subdued, sitting talking quietly to Gimlet. Glyn and Tomos were there and Molly was pouring tea she had just made.

"We've all been interviewed by the police again," Glyn explained.

"But why you, Dad?" Lydia asked, seeing the worried expression on her father's face.

"I knew her, see, and they're saying I was the last person to see her. That came out in the earlier inquiry when the family tried to find her. Sixteen years it is, mind, and they expect me to remember every detail, trying to trip me up and accusing me, if not of lying, then of being evasive."

"Gimlet too," Molly whispered. "It seems to me they were having a bit of a fling with the poor girl. Sounds like she was living off the streets."

"What did you say?" Matthew had been close enough to hear the whispered words and he took hold of Molly as if to shake her.

Tomos jumped up and threatened Matthew. "Take you hands off her. It's well known that Rosie was a tart. Memories aren't that short. What are you trying to make out, that she was pure and innocent? Found near a cache of jewellery wasn't she? Sounds like a falling out of thieves to me!"

"Leave it, Tomos," Glyn said quietly. "The man's got enough to cope with. Come on, Matthew. Let Molly alone, it isn't her fault. Gossip takes a long time to die."

Matthew released Molly and his shoulders drooped.

"I know she was fond of men. I wasn't such a child I didn't realise that, but it seems wrong to talk about it now, while she's there in the mortuary being studied like a jigsaw puzzle, while men try to make sense of her death."

"I'm sorry," Tomos said quietly, "but it's best to face it before the papers spread it all. You can imagine how they'll make a story out of this."

"All right. So Rosie was a prostitute!" Matthew turned on Billy and Gimlet. "Is that how you two knew her?"

Billy looked at his daughter. His face was almost as stricken as Matthew's. "You might as well know, Lydia, the police got it out of me tonight and tomorrow that will be all over the papers too," Billy said in a shaking voice. He pushed the door, afraid that Annie might hear. "I want to keep this from your Mam, mind. Right? I met Rosie over the allotments that night. She told me she was expecting a child and accused me of being the father. I laughed, told her I'd deny it and pushed her away."

"How did she die?" Lydia whispered.

"The police haven't said. But I pushed her and she tripped and fell and that's all I know. Scared I was that she'd tell your Mam. I walked away, angry with her for trying to get me involved in her trouble. But I swear she wasn't hurt. She sat there leaning back on her arms, swearing and shouting abuse till I reached the road and the sound of her had faded."

It was then, in the silence that followed Billy's confession, that Lydia realised that her father was a suspect.

Chapter Six

Lydia couldn't face Matthew knowing her father was implicated in the death of his sister. She went to work, returned home, dealt with the meals all as if she were a clockwork toy, wound up, faced in the right direction and programmed to perform.

Although she half expected to see him every time she went for her bus, and when she stepped off it each evening, there was no sign of him. She would hurry home, anxiously looking at the faces of those she passed, walk up the steps to her door, climb the stairs and enter the living room, then give a sigh of relief when he wasn't there. Another day's reprieve before she had to face him. Yet she knew that soon she must.

She presumed that the story of his sister's sordid death, spread over all the newspapers, had forced him to leave. She and Molly bore the brunt of it too, with people coming to the market stalls and buying something inexpensive just for the excuse to ask a lot of foolish questions.

So far, Annie had heard nothing. Shielded from the gossip by Billy and Lydia and, during the day, by Stella, she continued with her life without a worry, except the fear of being left alone for more than a brief interlude.

The inquest on Rosie Hiatt reopened and was again

postponed. The only surprise was the announcement that when she died she was four months pregnant. Rosie hadn't been lying about that.

The police visits trickled to a halt and for a few days Lydia began to relax, feeling that the awful business was at least put aside for a while and she could think about something else. She still saw Detective Superintentent Richards occasionally. He would call and stay for a cup of tea but he didn't question her, he seemed concerned for her and anxious to reassure her that eveything would settle down and her life would return to how he had been before the discovery of the body in its lonely grave.

"Memories are short for most people," he said. "Something else will happen and push this affair out of the limelight. But," he added, smiling kindly, "that won't happen until we get this lot sorted, so, if there's anything you think of, some small thing that you remember from that night, get in touch with me." He handed her a piece of paper bearing his name and telephone number. "You needn't go to the police station, just give me a ring and talk to me or leave a message with my wife. I'll help you deal with it with as little distress as possible."

She was grateful for his friendly interest and reassurance that, with the news coverage dying down, her father and Gimlet's notoriety would die down too. It was all so long ago. She began to feel her heart lightening, her frowns easing and was even making plans again for the opening of the wool shop.

Then, early one morning, there was a phone call.

"Keep your mouth shut if you want to live."

Wondering if it was some kind of joke, a half smile on her face, she listened for a moment, hearing only breathing at the other end then she asked the caller if he would repeat it. "So I can guess which of my idiot friends you are," she laughed.

"This isn't a joke, you stupid bitch! Keep your mouth shut about what happened at the castle. Right? And don't tell anyone or you'll end up like Rosie!"

She stared at the now buzzing instrument, still half convinced that it was some kind of joke, a sick joke, perhaps, but it couldn't be a serious threat. Could it? She stared at the phone for a while as if expecting it to give some explanation, then she quickly wrote down the words the person had uttered. Torn between believing it and trying to laugh and guess who it had been, she began to set the tray for her mother's breakfast with hands that trembled. Of course it was a joke. But who did she know who had that warped sense of humour?

She heard her father coming downstairs and hastily pushed the copy of the message under the tray. Best she said and did nothing until she'd had time to think about it. She knew anything that might be relevant to the death of Rosie Hiatt should be reported, but something held her back. Perhaps this wasn't anything to do with anything, just a silly idiot having a bit of fun at her expense.

Walking to the bus station an hour later she felt as if all eyes were upon her. Was the person on the phone watching her? Hoping she would reveal her fear? Defiantly she waved at Molly who came rushing up, late as usual and she laughingly described the joke caller's words, discussing in whispers the possibilities as to authorship.

Continuing with the same light-hearted mood, she told her employer, Mrs Thomas, and she told Glyn when he called at the stall later that morning.

"Lydia! You should have gone straight to the police!" he said anxiously. "The threat might be real! Not likely, though," he hastily reassured her, "but you should never take chances by presuming the most likely reason for something so potentially dangerous."

Glyn had begun the habit of calling either at the house or at the market stall each day to see how she was feeling. Although she had been glad of his company the night the body had been found, she felt it was time he stopped. His telling her what she should do about the call irritated her.

"All right, I'll talk to Superintendent Richards, but it will probably be a waste of his time!" she snapped.

"Shall I come with you?"

"No need. I intend going to see Matthew – I don't relish talking to him, I've been putting it off. With Dad involved in the enquiry about Rosie's death, he might not want to see me, but I have to try. I can't put it off any longer. Perhaps he'll come with me. It's more to do with him than you, even if it was us who found poor Rosie Hiatt. She was his sister."

"Sorry, Lydia, I know you think I'm interfering but I don't think you should tell anyone, not even Matthew, about the threatening call until the police have been told."

"Too late. I told Mrs Thomas and Molly. Laughed about it on the bus we did. So I expect half the village knows by now. Oh, and I told Tomos when he came to take Mam to Auntie Stella's," she added defiantly.

"That was foolish, Lydia." He spoke solemnly, so the words hung in the air.

"Too late now if it was," she retorted unrepentantly.

"Go now, take it to the police, I'll watch the stall for half an hour, Mrs Thomas won't mind and I haven't any pick-ups for a while."

"I'll go after work, with Matthew," she insisted.

Before going into the house she went to where Matthew was staying and after a few words of sympathy, which he brushed aside in his obvious delight at seeing her, she explained about the call.

"I've told several people," she told him. "I'm sure it's only some crank. But I don't want my parents worried by what's certain to be a juvenile attempt at a joke. Kids probably," she said. "Neville Nolan is quite capable of such a thing."

"I wish you hadn't told anyone, apart from me of course," Matthew said. "I agree with Glyn, you shouldn't take chances."

"You'll come with me to the police?"

"Let's go now and get it over with."

Richards wasn't there when they called at the station and she refused to discuss it with anyone else. As he had explained, it was simpler if she didn't have to repeat herself to several people.

"I'll walk you home," Matthew said.

"No need. I'll see you tomorrow." She touched her lips gently against his cheek, but he pulled her round until they were face to face and said softly,

"Oh Lydia, love. I missed you. I've been so afraid you'd have nothing more to do with me after all that's happened." He kissed her then, a slow, loving kiss. Staring into his deep-set eyes with another kiss hovering, Lydia forgot the fears and worries of the past days and lost herself in the thrill of a burgeoning love.

The phone was ringing insistently when she opened the door and she ran up the stairs to the living room two at a time exhilarated with the excitement of Matthew's kisses and the promise they offered of future happiness.

"That was foolish, Lydia," the voice said solemnly. "This is a last warning. Keep your pretty mouth shut!"

The words startled her out of her mood and brought her to earth with a sickening jolt. Besides the repeat of the threat was the horrifying realisation that the words and even the tone, were exactly what Glyn had said to her only a few hours previously. 'That was foolish, Lydia.'

Was it no more than a coincidence that both the anonymous caller and Glyn should utter the identical phrase?

Annie called down and asked for a cup of tea and Lydia stood there, distantly aware of the whining voice but not hearing it. This couldn't be happening. She had imagined it all. She started then, as there was a knock at the door.

She walked slowly down the stairs to the kitchen, her back sliding against the wall as if it offered protection. "Who is it?" she called.

"It's me, Matthew. I was worried so I came to see if you got home safely. Is everything all right, love?"

Lydia opened the door and practically threw herself on him with relief.

"Matthew, there's been another call, a warning like the first." She didn't tell him that the voice had repeated Glyn's words. She must have been mistaken about that.

"Don't go to the police," Matthew pleaded. "I think this person might be telling the truth and he does wish you harm. Forget it, say no more about the night you found Rosie, if you remember anything further don't

118

tell anyone, please, Lydia, promise me. There's more than my sister's death involved here and I don't think we should try finding out what it is."

"I have to tell them, now I've received a second one," she whispered. "I'm afraid to involve them, but more afraid not to."

"At least leave it for today," Matthew urged.

"But Superintendent Richards. He's sure to call and ask what I wanted."

"Make something up, but please don't say anything about this second call. I don't want to alarm you, but I think you should be careful."

"All right, but I don't feel very easy about going to Auntie Stella's as I planned. I think I'll stay in."

"Good! I'll be happier knowing you're safely inside. I'll meet you tomorrow morning and walk you to the bus, shall I?"

As soon as her parents were settled for the evening, Lydia's confidence returned. How foolish to imagine anyone would wish her harm! It was definitely some crank. Didn't cases like these always unearth a few? She would face her fear and walk to Auntie Stella's house.

Yet the fear did not completely dissolve and she had images of being followed, down the steps to the foreshore, along the dark streets, every doorway a threat.

She was wearing a dark cloak and feeling a bit stupid at her precautions. Her route took her up the hill away from the seafront before turning and making her way to the corner house that would soon be her corner shop.

Before she reached her aunt's gate a man called and she recognised the burly silhouette of Superintendent Richards against the lamp post opposite.

"I was hoping we'd meet," he said. "I understand you called at the station and asked for me earlier. Have you remembered anything more about the time you found the body?"

"No, I, er . . . I was just wondering if you'd found out how she died or whether there was any further news. I'm worried about Dad and Mr Howe."

"Of course you are." He appeared to accept her freshly invented story. "Come into the station, as we're so near and we can talk about it." He led her into a small room where a sketch of the castle kitchen had been drawn. Little squiggles were drawn in groups all over the area and Lydia asked what they were.

"They mark the places where someone had been digging," he said. "Remember it was here," he pointed to a large area of squiggles, that the body was found."

Lydia shook her head. "The turf had only been removed in two places, near the body and further over near the opposite wall," she insisted, pointing to the relevant places.

"Then you do know more than you've told us," the policeman said. His face as he stared at her was cold and threatening. "Not trying to cover for your father, are you?"

"But, I didn't try to keep that from you, I didn't know, until I saw the plan," she protested.

"All right, I believe you," he smiled "I know what a delicate instrument the memory can be. But if you remember anything else, I can't stress too heavily the importance of telling me." He touched the plan and explained. "Some of these lighter squiggles are areas where the ground had been disturbed previously but quite recently. We think our man had been going regulary to search for something and he was not certain about the hiding place."

"He was there, watching us, standing in the shadows while I stood looking down on that – that poor woman, wasn't he?"

"Maybe, or perhaps he went back, after you left, and dug further to find what he was looking for, and to take away his tools. They were borrowed from a shed in one of the allotments, by the way," he added. "From the way he dug, frantically, without the method he had previously used, he was searching for something – but not Rosie Hiatt. The way he drew attention to himself by panic makes it clear that was not what he expected to see when he pulled up that piece of turf."

"What was he looking for?"

"Evidence of those robberies? Or a weapon perhaps."

"D'you think he's dangerous, this mystery man?"

"He could be, if he's afraid of a prison sentence, and why else would he try and recover those things? Dangerous? I think it's possible. Why? What do you have to fear?" He looked at her and the expression on his face made her believe he could see into her mind and know she was not being completely truthful with him.

She told him then about the phone calls and he took notes and warned her to be extra careful. "But don't let this spoil your sleep, young lady. We'll be watching you. You can rely on that. Just go about your business as usual, don't let it worry you." In lighter tones he asked, "Is it true you're going to open a shop?"

"That's right, in my auntie's house, selling knitwear and wool."

"Put me down for a pair of hand-knitted woollen socks will you? I haven't had a pair since my mother died," he smiled. "My wife doesn't know how. Now," he stood up, dismissing her, "off we go, I'll walk you home, shall I?"

"No, I think I'll go and see my aunt."

Before he left her, at Stella's gate, he said, "Don't forget, if anything is worrying you, ring me. You have my number safe?" She nodded and he added, "If you don't want to phone, come and ask for me. You don't have to speak to anyone else, I know how confusing it can be explaining to half a dozen different people. Just keep me informed and I'll do the rest. Right? I don't want you to feel you're on your own in this."

He walked her along the quiet street near the gate of the castle grounds and she thanked him and knocked on her aunt's door, determinedly refusing to even glance up at the ruined castle on the sky line.

She didn't mention the phone calls to Stella, instead she forced her mind to concentrate on the new business. The order for their first stock of wool was due the following day and already knitting needles and patterns adorned the new shelves and walls of the front room. A second door, which had served the hairdressing salon, had been unblocked and on it hung the open/closed notice. Smilingly, Stella turned it to open then flicked it back again. "Won't be long now, will it?" she said.

As she did so there was a knock at the door and a face stared in at them. Stella squealed and Lydia gasped. It was a few seconds before they recognised Glyn.

"We're not even open yet!" Stella said, arms akimbo. "And anyway, it's after hours!"

"I saw you through the window and wondered if Lydia wanted company back home," he said when they opened the door to him.

"I'm all right, I don't need a nursemaid," Lydia replied but she didn't refuse. The streets were dark and with only a few people about, footsteps behind her could be very frightening.

"Did you go to the police?" he asked as they set off an hour later down the hill towards the seafront.

"I did and they weren't particularly worried," she told him flippantly. "It's a crank, sure to be. That's what that man Richards thinks. Cases like this always attract them."

"But they will keep an eye on you?"

"Of course they will but they don't really think it's necessary."

"I'm still driving for Tomos and I'll be watching too," Glyn replied. She tried to pretend she didn't value his concern, but she was reassured and pleased to know he would be watching out for her. With Glyn and Detective Superintendent Richards looking out for her, surely nothing could harm her?

In an attempt to revive interest in the death of Rosie Hiatt, the newspapers did an update on the investigation. There was still no clear evidence about how she died, and the mystery of the burial remained. Lydia saw her father studying the review of the case and she knew he was distressed.

"It will soon be over, Dad," she comforted. "Cheer up. No one has accused you of murder, have they? So don't look so tragic," she teased.

"You don't have to wield the weapon to be guilty, mind," he said sadly.

Lydia went to see to Gimlet and asked him to talk

123

her father out of his depressed mood. Gimlet looked thoughtful and promised to try.

On the allotments a few days later, Gimlet stood up from cleaning the dead plants from his bean sticks and saw Billy staring towards the top of the plots, near the trees that hid much of the castle from their view.

"Thinking about Rosie, are you?" he asked softly.

"I can't get her out of my mind," Billy replied sadly. "We all knew she was a tart, living off what men paid her but she didn't deserve to be killed and buried up there with no one to mourn her." He turned to look at Gimlet, distress distorting his features. "We used her and sneered at her as if we were better than she. I'm at least partly responsible, you know that, don't you?"

"I know that, Billy. Best you don't think too deeply over it. You didn't kill her and that's what you must remember."

"I did kill her – oh, I didn't murder her, but she came to me that night and I turned her away, refused to help. She wasn't seen again. If I'd had even a little sympathy, damn it all, man, I wouldn't turn a wounded cat away, yet I turned my back on her, an eighteen year old child. I might as well have killed her. I drove her to whoever did."

"Suicide it was," Gimlet said quietly.

"That would be worse. If I walked away when she was so desperate, what's that if it isn't killing her? Besides, it couldn't have been suicide. She was buried and she couldn't have buried herself."

"I buried her, Billy."

"You what?" Billy turned and stared at Gimlet as if he were a stranger.

"When I met you that night, after you'd spoken to her, I was worried. It was in The Pirate. Remember?"

124

"I remember. I was scared she would tell Annie we'd been seeing each other. She just told me she was going to have a baby and it was mine."

"You said she staggered and fell when you shook her and told her you wouldn't be responsible for her child."

"I was so angry. Annie was ill and Lydia only a child. I couldn't let her ruin their lives. You understand, don't you?"

"I was worried," Gimlet repeated, "so I went to find her."

"Unhurt she was. Shouting at me as I walked away."

"She was lying there, on the spot you've been staring at for so long and look at every time we come here. That was where you'd left her, wasn't it?" Billy nodded, still staring at his friend. "There was blood on her face," Gimlet went on, "and I could see at once that she was dead. It was only after I'd started to run away, and returned for a second look, that I realised her wrists had been cut."

"I didn't hurt her, I swear to you," Billy said urgently. "If I'd known she was so desperate I'd have done something, I'd have thought of some way to help her."

"It wasn't shaking her and causing her to fall that killed her Billy, that was why I did what I did. I carried her up through the trees to the castle, climbed in the way we kids had always got inside, and left her there. I put my coat over her, wrapped her up warm just in case. Later, almost dawn it was, I went back and buried her. I – I knew she was dead, that first time I looked at her. It was obvious her life was ended but I was afraid, what if I was wrong? So I left her to make sure, then I dug a grave and left her there."

125

"You did that for me?"

"Pals we are, and both of us involved with the poor girl. You'd have done the same if I'd been the one in trouble."

"But never to say a word, all these years."

"I didn't feel any guilt for what I did. I knew you hadn't killed her and there wasn't any point in you suffering remorse, probably having to admit to Annie what had been going on, and ruining little Lydia's childhood. It seemed for the best."

"What can I say?"

"Buy me a pint, boy and forget this conversation ever took place."

"The police seem convinced she was involved in some robberies and the death was due to a falling out."

"That's what they're saying and best if we accept it."

Both men were subdued that evening as they sat at their usual table in The Pirate. Although Gimlet pleaded with Billy not to discuss it any more in case a hint of what happened escaped and ruined his years of silence, Billy's mind wouldn't leave it alone.

"That man who was digging up there, what could he have been after?"

"The police found a jacket that had been wrapped around a gun. Someone trying to find it before the workmen found it perhaps? It was used in a robbery, or at least, that what the papers are saying. There were stolen goods up there too, the thief might have come back to find that. Medals as well as jewellery, some belonging to the Franks who young Molly lives with. Funny to think of things like that going on in our own little village, isn't it?"

"The police have dug up all the kichen area and

across the courtyard. They've searched through the dungeons too, opening up a room that's been half buried for centuries, but they found nothing."

"You don't think it could have been Matthew Hiatt, do you? That somehow, after all this time he'd learnt the truth about his sister's disappearance and came back here to look for her?"

"It is a bit of a coincidence, him turning up here at this time. But, coincidences do happen."

"They do, and sometimes, I even believe them," Billy replied cynically.

Annie knew there was something worrying Billy and in her usual unhappy way she presumed his subdued mood was something that would cast a shadow on her own wellbeing. Perhaps he was fed up with caring for her, although he was his usual attentive self, coming to see her as soon as he returned from work and climbing the stairs without complaint if she called down for something. He still smiled at her but the smile was hollow and she dreaded him telling her something serious.

He wasn't ill, she was reasonably certain of that. He slept easily and his appetite wasn't impaired by whatever was taking the glow from his blue eyes. She waited every time she saw him for him to tell her the problem, but when nothing was said, she dared not ask. If it was something that would affect her badly she would rather not know until the telling was unavoidable.

She reached out for one of the sweets Stella brought her. Boiled sweet she usually had but today Stella had given her some chocolate brazils, a real treat, and she stopped with the chocolate touching her lips and frowned. Was this treat to relax her, make her happy and better able to stand bad news? She chewed slowly, frowning slightly as she pondered over the week's happenings to try and fathom what the problem could be.

She was so deeply in thought that at first the sound didn't penetrate her mind. First the slightest of creaks as the back door opened, then the kitchen door knob turning. It was the slight draught that finally made her stop chewing and listen.

Automatically she glanced at the clock beside her bed. Too early for Billy, and Stella was at the shops and wouldn't be back for another half an hour. It must be Lydia. Unwell perhaps? Was that what was creating the atmosphere of gloom? Was Lydia unwell and they not wanting to tell her and cause her to worry?

Her flesh began to creep as she realised that if it had been any of her family they wouldn't be creeping in so silently. Although she often dozed during the day, none of them worried about waking her. They called the moment they entered the kitchen. Whoever had come into the house was making as little noise as possible so had no right to be there. And she was alone in the house.

She held her breath, spitting out the nut she had been about to eat, and listened intently. Someone was coming upstairs. One by one she heard the stairs creak. The draught was still disturbing the air so whoever it was had left the door open, ready to make his escape. Along the landing now. Then she knew without doubt that the intruder was standing outside her door.

Too terrified to move she wrapped her arms around her chest and stared as the door slowly closed and the key was turned. She called then, her voice croaky and weak.

"Lydia? Is that you? Why are you locking the door?" Then louder, "Who is it? What d'you want? My husband will be back in a minute, mind!" She began to sob then, deep throbbing groans that revealed the extent of her distress. Someone was playing a trick on her, and her in bed, a sick woman. "Who is it?" she wailed. "Open this door. Please, open the door, I'm choking."

She didn't hear the intruder unlock the door nor his footsteps as he ran back down the stairs, and she was still sobbing when the door opened and Stella appeared.

Stella was alarmed, hearing the crying, then, on opening the bedroom door, seeing her sister in such a state. Annie's face was wet with perspiration, her hair sticking up and wild. The covers had been strewn across the floor and Annie was panting, holding her throat as if she were choking.

"Annie! Love! Whatever's the matter?" Stella ran to her and poured a drink of water from the jug on the bedside table. Annie's arms flayed out and knocked it from her hand without drinking. Stella tried to calm the woman, sitting beside her on the bed and holding her still. After a few moments she felt her relax and the sobbing became a subdued whine. Stella patted her as if she were soothing a baby, wondering what could have happened to get her in such a state. It was months, years since this had been a regular occurance.

"Now, tell me what happened," she coaxed, as she wiped Annie's face with a cool flannel and continued to calm her. "Only out for half an hour I was, stopped to chat to some friends. I have to get out sometimes, Annie. Billy will be back soon. And Lydia. You'll have them both back before you know it."

"There was someone here," Annie whispered.

"There can't have been, love. I was only gone a little while."

"He came up the stairs and stood outside my door."

"Nonsense, you've had a bad dream that's all. Look how hot you are, a nightmare you've had. I keep telling you to keep a window open, this room gets too hot."

"Stella, listen to me. He came in, stood there by the door and locked me in."

"But the door wasn't locked when I came back. How could he have locked you in?"

After a while, although she didn't believe Annie had experienced anything more frightening than a bad dream, Stella pretended to believe her and after washing her, getting her a fresh nightdress and settling her once more in bed, she sat and waited for Billy to return from his drink with Gimlet.

Lydia was home first, having cancelled a planned visit to the cinema and spent a couple of hours with Molly instead. When she was told what had happened she was worried.

"What if she was telling the truth?" she whispered to her aunt. "What if someone to do with Rosie Hiatt thinks I know more than I've told and has been here searching for something? Oh, Auntie Stella, I'm frightened."

For the second time that night Stella had to soothe an agitated relative! This time she wasn't so gentle.

"Oh come on, Lydia, don't you start going crazy on me! Your mam had a bad dream and that's all there is to it. Now, I'll get a sandwich made shall I? Your dad is usually starving when he and Gimlet have had a couple of hours of putting the world to rights." Her common sense approach did what she hoped and made Lydia realise how unlikely it was that someone had been in their home.

Lydia wanted to go straight upstairs and investigate her bedroom to make sure nothing had been touched but she didn't. No point in frightening her mother more by revealing that she accepted the possibility of an intruder. She went to check that her mother was all right, leaving the bedroom door open so Annie could hear the buzz of conversation and be reassured that there was someone there. For a while at least they had better not leave her alone in the house, even for half an hour. She wondered with a stab of panic what her chances of a normal life would be if Auntie Stella grew tired of giving so generously of her time.

"I'm so grateful to you," she said when she went back down to where Stella was preparing a plate of sandwiches.

"No fuss. I'm her sister after all."

"But you do so much and I'm afraid we don't tell you often enough how much you're valued."

"Pass the cheese and stop making me feel embarrassed. I do it because I love you, you're my family, all of you."

By the time Billy came in, the house was calm. Stella explained what had happened and he ran straight up to his wife but returned immediately. Annie was fast asleep. Like Stella he thought it was nothing more than a dream. "But," he said with a glance at Lydia, "just in case, I'll put the bolt on the back door when we go to bed, just in case, eh?"

"Yes, just to reassure Mam." Lydia smiled.

When her father left to walk Stella home, calling for her to bolt the door after them, Lydia went to her room and stared at it as if she hadn't seen it before.

131

Books on every surface, including the bed itself. There were catalogues and invoices, and advertizing placards, together with samples of wools, colour cards, files, lists of suppliers and lots more clutter all dealing with the new business, spread around the room making it look nothing like the normally tidy room she inhabited.

If someone had been here, where would he have looked? What was he looking for? She had no connection with Rosie Hiatt, why would anyone think she had? Yet she still stared around hoping for a clue to why someone had entered their home, in spite of her reassurances to Stella, she had a firm belief that her mother hadn't been mistaken.

Annie was sick, keeping to her room for so much of her time, but she had never shown any hint of an over-active imagination. And a dream, well surely once you woke from a dream it faded into memory faster than a blink? Annie's description had been so detailed.

The books spread about so untidily she ignored, and looked instead at the drawers and cupboards, sifting carefully for a sign they had been disturbed. After several minutes she shrugged. Since she had begun the preparations for opening the wool shop she had been anything but tidy. How would she know amid this mess if a dozen people had been there?

She undressed and sat on the bed, waiting for her father to return so she could unbolt the door for him. She was very tired. The extra work and the worries about the shop were beginning to tell. "Hurry up," she murmured to her absent father. "I'll fall asleep if you aren't back soon." Her eyes closed and she forced them open and let them wander aimlessly around the room, hardly seeing anything, just trying to stay awake to hear her father's first gentle knock. Then she saw it and at once all tiredness fled.

On the corner cupboard was a notepad that hadn't been there before. With shaking hands she picked it up and read:

'Keep away from the police, or you'll regret it, and so will your mother.'

Chapter Seven

It was Stella who told Glyn about the night Annie had been frightened. He had guessed something was wrong. When he saw Lydia she was very nervous, glancing around as if aware of someone watching her. He asked her repeatedly what was wrong but she always smiled and insisted there was nothing. Determined to find out what was worrying her, he had asked Stella.

"I don't think for a minute that it was true, mind," she said after explaining about finding Annie in a state convinced she had heard someone in the house and been locked in her room.

"And Lydia agreed that it was nothing more than her mother's over-active imagination?"

"Well, let's be honest, Glyn. My sister Annie isn't a saint. She has us all running round after her and when she's been left alone, even for a short while, she does play up and try to make us feel guilty."

"You think that's all it was then?"

"I can't think of anything else, love. Surely Lydia didn't really believe someone had been in the house, locked Annie in, then unlocked the door and run away without robbing the place or even staying more than a couple of minutes? What sense is there in that?"

"You are sure it was nonsense? No one had been

in had they? Nothing taken? Did you check all the rooms?"

"Billy, Lydia and I checked downstairs and in the bedrooms. Lydia looked in her room while Billy and I checked downstairs again. We didn't find a thing out of place. Everything was just as we'd left it. Nothing was missing or one of us would have noticed for sure."

"And nothing had been moved? There wasn't anything there that shouldn't have been?"

"A burglar who brings something instead of taking something away? Now there's a novelty!"

When Glyn called to take Annie to Stella's the following day. Annie handed him the key and told him to, "Lock up secure, mind! I don't want to come home again and find someone in the house. Terrible shock that was, and knowing no one believes me makes it worse."

"I believe you," Glyn said. "And I think Lydia does too. She's been nervous ever since."

"Sorry I am that she's been frightened but I had to tell someone. I can't get it out of my mind."

"Tell *me* then, it might help if you talk about it."

"I was sitting on the bed crouched and terrified, listening as someone came up the stairs. The door knob was turned and my door was pulled shut. The key snapped and I was locked in. I don't know how long afterwards that Stella came back, not more than ten minutes I suppose, but before she did the key snapped again." She swallowed nervously. "There's loud it sounded, the key turning in the silence of the house." She shivered at the memory, clinging to his arm as they reached the pavement and he helped her into the taxi. "Then," she went on, "footsteps running down the stairs. Not loud, mind, the man was trying

135

not to be heard. What could he have wanted, Glyn? He didn't take anything, Billy and Lydia and Stella made sure nothing had been taken."

When he left her at Stella's, where the final touches were being done to the displays in the shop, Glyn drove to his next pickup looking very thoughtful.

The market in the town was transformed. From attractive and neatly displayed stalls selling every kind of food and a wide variety of other goods, the approach of Christmas had made it less functional and given the whole place a party mood. Every stallholder had done their best to make the place attractive, each vying with neighbours to give the customers the finest spectacle.

The expression on children's faces made their work worthwhile and many were reminded that if some adults swore that Christmas was a sham, for the children, seeing the colourful exhibitions through their innocent eyes, it was a magical time.

Lydia loved Christmas and every aspect gave her pleasure but today she was unable to concentrate on her work. The customers, whom she normally enjoyed helping to make their choice from the market stall's wide selection, were a trial. She wanted to be home, locked in the house where she felt safe, or with Stella, getting the shop ready for customers and forcing her mind away from the thought of an intruder.

"Why don't you go home?" Molly said. "Fat lot of good you are here. Ring Mrs Thomas and tell her you're ill."

"But I'm not ill."

"Pale as milk, heavy-eyed, and walking around like a weary sleep-walker? I call that a reason for saying you're ill and getting yourself off home!"

"I haven't slept very well, I keep thinking I can hear someone trying to break in," she admitted.

"If anyone wanted to break in, they wouldn't do it at night while the three of you were there, now would they?"

At eleven o'clock Lydia was persuaded, and once Mrs Thomas came and agreed that she was not well enough to work, she went to the bus station and thankfully headed for home.

She smiled as she remembered Molly's insistence that she didn't stay on the stall, then her friend's words came back and alarmed her. "If anyone wanted to break in, they wouldn't do it at night while the three of you were there . . ." No, they would choose a time when the house was empty, like now! Suddenly she was afraid to enter the house. It was no longer a haven, a place of safety. On the steps leading up from the foreshore, she stopped and looked up at the windows. The back window was her bedroom, where she had always felt comfortable. Was there someone inside this minute, searching through her things?

Slowly she opened the door. It wasn't locked! Mam must have forgotten again, she thought with irritation. She'd been so badly frightened, had upset them all, then forgot to lock the door! She went through the small kitchen and up the stairs. A sound alerted her and she stopped and pressed herself against the wall. It was coming from her bedroom. In trepidation she climbed the second flight of stairs, her heart beating painfully in her throat. She was terrified at what she might find but she couldn't not go. To flee, to turn her back on this threat was impossible. She reached the doorway and cautiously looked into the room.

For a moment she didn't believe what she was seeing, and she stood in her doorway staring at the intruder with anger mounting by the split-second.

He was standing beside her bed examining a small package.

"Glyn! What are you doing?"

Startled, he dropped the package and stuffed it out of sight under the bed covers, which had been thrown back as if he had been searching through her bedding.

"It was *you* who came here and frightened Mam! What are you looking for? Tell me what you want and you can have it. You don't have to break in and skulk around, we'll give it to you!" She was trembling with the anti-climax of seeing Glyn and not some unknown thief. The relief increased her anger.

"Lydia! You gave me a fright. I didn't expect you home."

"That much is obvious! Get out! And think yourself lucky I'm not calling the police!"

Glyn took the two steps necessary to reach her and held her shoulders, making her look at him. "Lydia, I'm not trying to steal anything and it was not me who came and locked your mother's door. I forgot to give your mother back her key when I locked up and I took the opportunity of looking, in the hope that I might find something that you missed. Something that might give a clue to what's going on. You're involved in something and I want to find out what it is."

"Very convincing!" She pushed past him and grabbed at the covers, pulling them back and revealing the object he had been studying. The rather battered cardboard box, which she quickly opened, contained a selection of beribboned medals.

"How convincing are you about these?" she

demanded. "They're the medals the police are looking for aren't they?"

"Yes, I think they might be."

"And you were going to hide them here?"

"No, Lydia! It isn't what it seems. I was looking for – I don't know what – I was just hoping that if your mother really heard someone in the house, that I'd see something that you had missed. I guessed that the intruder must have come, not to take something, but to bring something, and I found this box. I had to look inside as I had no idea whether or not it was yours. It isn't, is it?"

"No, of course not."

"From the robberies is my guess and as such these medals would be incriminating if they were found on the thief, so he hid them in your room." His voice slowed as he realised she didn't believe him. "Go on, call the police. I'll tell them exactly where I found them."

"And where was that?" She was trying hard not to believe him. It would have been so easy to accept what he said. Far easier than telling herself that Glyn Howe, a man she had known all her life, a man she was still half in love with, was a thief and possibly worse.

"They were hidden in one of your summer sandals, tucked in between them in the shoe-rack in your wardrobe."

"Not a very clever hiding place."

"You didn't find them. And I don't suppose he meant to leave them there for very long. Just until he could either sell them or dispose of them safely." He stared at her. Her lovely face was troubled as she fought against believing him. He knew she would want to believe him, but would try and remain neutral, not wanting to be his partner even in a conviction of his innocence. He had hurt her so badly and it saddened him more each time he looked at her.

"Why would he hide them here?" he asked. "Tell me, who's been in the house since the incident at the castle?"

"I haven't any reason to think they were hidden here! I haven't seen them before and Dad and I searched this room thoroughly after Mam's fright."

"Did you take your shoes out of the rack?"

"Why am I answering *your* questions? You should be answering mine!"

"Tell me, who's been here?"

"Molly, Tomos, your father, and *you*! Which one do I suspect? The one I found trying to hide this!" She waved the box at him angrily.

"You shouldn't have touched it, not without gloves, there might have been fingerprints," he said.

"How clever of you to mention that – after I'd picked it up and opened it, examined it and made sure my prints were all over it! Covering yours? Was that your reason, Glyn?"

"Tried and found guilty am I?"

She sank down on the bed, her shoulders slumped. "Glyn, I don't want to think you had anything to do with this affair, but what am I to think? You come out of the Navy, tell me you no longer want to marry me. You talk about a girlfriend whom you never see, or hear from. Now I find you with stolen goods and, worst of all, trying to hide them in my bedroom."

"It isn't what it seems," he insisted again.

"I've made up my mind, I'm phoning Detective Superindendent Richards. He'll get to the truth, I'm not sure I can."

Glyn didn't reply. He was looking across to the corner of the room where the large brass-bound box had been placed. "I looked in there," he said softly. "All those things, they were for us, weren't they? Pillowcases, sheets, cutlery and china. All for our home."

"History, Glyn Howe," she said firmly. "They'll stay there in case I decide to find a flat of my own. Handy they'll be if I do. They won't be wasted and they aren't causing me any distress seeing them there. It's glad I am that I've escaped from a man I thought I knew but who's surrounded in mystery. I don't like mysteries, Glyn. Never did."

"I found this too," he said as if she hadn't spoken. He opened her wardrobe door and pulled out a man's jacket. Expensive but grubby. "Matthew's isn't it? Been here, in your room, has he?"

"No he hasn't. Not that it's any business of yours! I promised to mend the sleeve and fix a loose button. Anything else you want to know?"

"Yes. Can I have a cup of coffee?"

"Get out!"

"Not until I make you believe that I was only here to try and help."

"To make sure I don't go to the police, more like!"

"I've no fear of that, but I think it's best to keep things as quiet as possible, it might be safer that way. Whoever came here that night, he wouldn't want much encouragement to come again if he failed to find what he was looking for, or, if he knew we'd found what he had hidden."

Lydia put the jacket back in the wardrobe and went down to make coffee. Her mind was a jumble of half thought-out facts. How could she accept that the body at the castle and the robbery connected with it had something to do with Glyn? That

141

sort of thing didn't happen. It simply did not happen.

When she was calmer, she decided that for the moment she would accept Glyn's word that he was searching for, and not planting something. But the medals had obviously been left there by someone and Glyn pleaded with her not to mention their discovery to the police.

"You could be in danger," he said, looking at her, trying desperately to convince her. "I don't know what went on at the castle, but somehow you're involved, possibly only because you and I found the body of Rosie Hiatt and went to the police. Please, love, don't tell anyone, we'll get rid of the medals somehow and try and forget the whole nasty business."

After a serious discussion on the best and safest way of disposing of the the medals, they decided to send them back to the police anonymously.

"What about returning them via the local paper? That way we'd make sure their return was publicised," Glyn explained. "Then the thief, whoever he is, will know that they are no longer here and he'll have no reason to break in to get them back." Lydia nodded agreement.

"We tell no one, right?" Glyn added firmly.

Again, she agreed, but there was a residue of doubt. She was not fully convinced by Glyn's explanations, but wanted an end to it and, involving the papers in the return of the medals might just achieve that.

The tall man was angry. He stood looking up at Lydia's window in the darkness. The news on the local paper about the medals being returned had been headline news that evening. There had been no mention of them being found in Lydia's bedroom so it was unlikely that the police were watching the place, but he knew from previous experience that the police didn't always impart all their information.

Contrary to Molly's opinion, he did go in at night. The bolt had fortunately been forgotten and the lock gave him little trouble. He went up the stairs with hardly a sound. Through the living room and up the stairs, he stopped and listened at Annie and Billy's room and heard the soft breathing that told him they were sleeping. Then, moving like a shadow to the room where Lydia slept, he stepped inside and stood for a moment looking down at her sleeping peacefully. He wasn't in the room for more than thirty seconds and came out carrying Matthew's jacket.

Telling Molly was essential. If Lydia didn't talk to someone about her fears she felt she would explode! She explained about finding Glyn searching her room and the discovery of the medals.

"He must be telling the truth," Lydia said. "I can't really see Glyn Howe in the role of thief and I certainly can't see him digging holes and burying the body of a local prostitute when he was little more than a child! No, we have to believe him. So, who did put the medals in my room, and why?"

"He must have thought it the safest place."

"Yes, I suppose it was a good choice. Although the police still question Dad from time to time and fill his mind with panic at the thought of being arrested, they aren't likely to search my room again. If they did find it they would look to my father for explanations, wouldn't they?" Lydia shivered at the thought of her father being further implicated.

"They've probably lost interest, unless you tell them about finding the medals, that is. And," she added thoughtfully, "it was Glyn who talked you out of that, wasn't it Lydia?"

Lydia and Matthew continued to meet and it was almost impossible not to discuss the events of the past weeks. He asked if there was any news, although, being the brother of the victim, he was able to make enquiries himself. As always it was she who did most of the talking. "Trying to persuade him to tell me what the police told him, was like drawing teeth!" she told Molly. "I don't think he does it deliberately, he just isn't a chatterbox like most of us."

"Best you behave the same, Lydia," Molly warned. "Lovely he is and I know you're getting very fond of him, but he is only here for a few more weeks and he hasn't said anything about what happens then."

"He's fond of me too," Lydia defended.

The two friends were sitting in Stella's front room, now a smart new shop. Molly had called to see how the work was progressing and was waiting, unknown to Lydia, until the time she had arrranged to meet Tomos. Although Lydia knew the affair was continuing the girls rarely discussed it.

The shelves had been admired and the displays discussed and conversation had dwindled. Both girls were thinking of Tomos, Molly anticipating their meeting with excitement, and Lydia contemplating the end of Tomos and Melanie's marriage with some sadness. So, when someone knocked on the shop door they were both startled to see Melanie standing there. Molly's instinct was to run. Lydia felt her face colour expecting this to be a confrontation, with Melanie demanding that Molly stay away from her husband. But the expression of Melanie's face was without anger. With some trepidation, Lydia let her in.

"The shop isn't open yet, Melanie. Not till Monday."

"I only wanted a word," Melanie said, glancing at Molly as if hoping she would leave. "In private, like."

"Just off." Molly slipped on her coat and left by the shop door, calling to Stella as she closed the shop door behind her.

"It's about Tomos," Melanie said, and Lydia's heart gave a lurch. This was it. The affair between Tomos and Molly had been discovered. She took a deep breath then asked, "Tomos? Not ill, is he?"

"No, but there's something wrong."

"In what way, Melanie?" Lydia was going to stall as long as she could.

"That's the trouble, I don't know. He spends a lot of time away from the house."

"Meeting the boys for sure. Nothing more likely than that. Glyn and he still keep in touch with their mates, don't they? You don't mind him having a little drink, do you? I don't think you'll cure him of meeting his friends for a drink and a gossip. Worse than women they are." Lydia knew she was gabbling, but she had to delay Melanie asking the one question she was dreading. She'd have to lie and that didn't come easily to her.

"I think he's gambling," Melanie said. "I think he's spending hours in people's houses playing cards and gambling."

It was such a relief Lydia almost laughed aloud.

"The trouble is," Melanie went on, "I don't know where he's getting the money. He works fewer and fewer hours, giving Glyn all the time he asks for, so where is he getting the money?"

"Have you thought that he could be winning?"

This time Lydia did allow herself a chuckle. "They don't all lose do they? Perhaps he makes enough to cover his needs in a few hours and gives the rest of the work to Glyn, knowing how desperate he is to earn it?"

"The business should be more important than a few card games. Why is he losing interest like this?"

"Why don't you ask him?" Lydia asked.

"I can't. You see," Melanie added softly, "I'm half afraid that he's having an affair and not gambling after all. What would I do then?" She hesitated a moment then added, "You would tell me if he was, wouldn't you, Lydia?"

The words Lydia had been dreading had been spoken. She was so undecided about what to say, her thoughts scattered and she pretended a cough to give herself time to calm down. Melanie was a friend of sorts; related they'd have been if she and Glyn had married. But Molly was also a friend, for as far back as her memory would go.

"What would I do?" Melanie repeated mournfully.

"Kick him up the backside, and out of the house so fast his feet will catch fire!"

"That's the problem. It's his parents' house. It would be me who'd have to go. I'd come out of this marriage with nothing to show for the years. Back to my family, back home to Mam and Dad. What a come-down. I don't think I could face that, Lydia."

Lydia's mind jumped. Her immediate thought was not sympathy for Melanie or for Molly and Tomos in the mess they had made of their lives, but for herself. She knew so little about Matthew. What if he were married and she became 'the other woman'? She

146

abandoned her plans to work and instead, closed the shop and took Melanie to a cafe for a coffee and the largest cream cake they could find. She had no solutions to offer, only more puzzles.

Matthew spent a lot of his time walking the hills and cliffs around the coast and Lydia would occasionally receive a postcard explaining where he was and how soon he would return. He always turned up when he promised and their reunions were blissful. He would bring a present, and for a short time he would be full of talk of places he'd seen and people he'd met and small adventures he'd had. She was reminded of the way she and Glyn were when he had leave from the Navy. It almost made the partings worthwhile, but not quite.

For the first evening, usually spent at a restaurant with good food and good wine, he would chatter animatedly, then as the evening reached its end, he would withdraw again into the uncommunicable young man she was beginning to love. He still lived at the same small hotel on the seafront, but rarely invited her there. He explained that it was rather shabby and not the sort of place he wanted to spend their time together. She didn't question this, it was all a part of the quality of his attention. "Nothing but the best," he told her. "Nothing but the best for my best girl."

As he had during the time he walked in the Brecon Beacons, when Rosie's body was found, he carried a small one-man tent on his travels and ate in cafés or built a fire and cooked something from the supplies in his rucksack.

"I could live like this indefinitely," he told her one day. "Pity of it is that I have to earn money. At least

147

teaching gives me more time to enjoy the freedom of the hills, and it's then I'm most happy."

"Not when you're with me?" she teased and he smiled that special smile, his deep-set eyes glowing with what she suspected, and hoped, was the beginnings of a lasting love. She almost envied him his casual and easy existence, but not completely. The idea sounded romantic and when he invited her to go with him one weekend she was tempted, "But," she explained, "I don't think I'd feel very happy sleeping in a tent, I find the house frightening enough at present."

"Why is that?" he asked. And that was when she forgot caution and told him all that had happened.

He listened quietly, watching her and nodding occasionally but not interupting. Then he smiled and said, "So, that's why you've been evasive when I've asked for the return of my jacket?"

"Who could have taken it, Matthew? It was a good one but even so, breaking in and taking a jacket no one could have expected to find? I don't wear men's jackets and my father, well, you know how casually he dresses, I don't think he's owned one for years."

"A tramp? Why look for a complicated explanation when a simple one is more likely? He probably didn't need to go any further than the living room."

"It was hanging in my wardrobe."

"You probably forgot where you left it. Wasn't it in the living room beside the sewing box ready for mending? An opportunist thief could have come in, seen it and taken it. There's a lot of winter left for those sleeping rough."

"I have a good memory, Matthew, and I definitely didn't leave it in the living room. It was in my wardrobe. Certain of that I am."

"Talking about memory, have you remembered anything else about the night my sister was found?"

She shook her head. "That policeman, Richards, still calls occasionally but I think he's just being kind, and making sure I've recovered from that awful night. No, I don't think there's anything else. I'd have remembered before now." But in this she was wrong.

The shop opened to business the following Monday morning. Tomos had called to take Annie to Stella's as usual but this time, Lydia went with them. There was a bunch of flowers on the taxi seat when she helped her mother in and Annie took them and smiled. "These for me then?" she asked.

"No, Annie, they're for your daughter. A good luck wish from me and our Glyn." Tomos took the flowers from Annie and handed them to Lydia with a bow. "Good luck, love, and," he added in a whisper, "thanks for stalling with Melanie the other day."

"I didn't want to," Lydia said grimly. "I feel sorry for her and I think you should tell her and get things sorted before she finds out from someone else. Cruel that would be and whatever you and she feel – or don't feel – for each other, Melanie doesn't deserve that!" The flowers no longer gave her pleasure and as soon as she went inside, she threw them into the dustbin. She didn't want thanks for lying to someone over something that should have been settled months ago!

In spite of the sour start, the day went well. Several people came to buy wool and patterns and many more came to see what "Lydia Jones, Quality Knitwear and Wool", intended to stock. Lydia had a fright when she saw Superintendent Richards coming in, but he was

149

smiling and his visit was purely innocent of worries. He simply ordered three pairs of hand-knitted socks from Stella. Glyn came to put the finishing touches to a glass-fronted shelf he had made, and invited her out for a snack at one o'clock. She refused.

"I have to go shopping to get something for dinner, and besides, Auntie Stella and I want to discuss the morning's business," she told him briskly. To Stella, she said, "Glyn can keep his lunch. It would probably be a small bag of chips anyway, that's all he can afford these days, in spite of working every moment he can."

"He worked here for nothing, remember," Stella reminded her. "Sundays, and evenings after Annie left. He said he didn't want to disturb her with the banging and sawing and drilling. Thoughtful of him. He's a very kind man, Glyn Howe. I just hope that whatever it is that's bothering him will soon be sorted."

"What's bothering him is this woman he's found! Making him work and provide a house for her she is. I was prepared for us to start off in Mam and Dad's front bedroom, so he could invest in his family's business, but that wasn't good enough for him, was it?"

"You do believe in this Cath, then?"

"Oh, I don't know what to believe. I only know that it no longer concerns me!"

When Tomos brought Billy to collect Annie and take her home that first day, Lydia didn't go with them. "I'll be back as soon as I can, but I want to check on a few things first," she told her father. It was as they were clearing a space ready for a new delivery they were expecting the following day, that Lydia found Glyn's wallet.

150

"Look at this! I wonder who it belongs to? It's a man's wallet by the look of it. Perhaps Tomos dropped it when he carried Mam through?" She opened it to see if there was anything to identify the owner and saw that it belonged to Glyn. Unable to resist, she pulled out some papers, and a bank statement was among them. His account held over ten thousand pounds.

Chapter Eight

Lydia was both alarmed and angry on discovering that Glyn, who was working so hard and insisting he was short of money, had ten thousand pounds in a bank account. She was tempted to tell him she knew, face him with it to see if he would explain. Then she accepted the fact sadly that it was no longer her business. He had said goodbye and announced that he had fallen in love with someone else, so what he did was no longer of any concern to her. Although with the burglaries of sixteen years ago being re-investigated, and the uneasy suspicion that he was somehow involved, there was an air of anxiety about the discovery that he owned such a large sum of money.

"Best you say nothing," Stella advised. "No fault on him if he's saving hard. There's nothing terrible about a man working and saving for something he wants bad, now is there?"

Unconvinced, Lydia nodded and tried to dismiss the vision of the bank statement from her mind. Besides being startled to know how much he had saved, it was also hurtful. The money he had put aside had been intended for their future home, hers and Glyn's. To know it was being spent on another woman, someone she hadn't met and knew nothing about, made disappointment add fresh pain.

She relived the awful homecoming and the evening when he had walked in and told her he no longer wanted to marry her. She had to force herself back from tears that burned to be shed.

"I'll take it to him on the way home," Lydia said, throwing the hateful object down on the counter.

"Shall I take it?" Stella offered. "He needn't know you saw anything. I'll tell him it was me who found it and looked inside for the owner, shall I?"

Lydia shook her head. "No, I think I'd enjoy him knowing that I'd seen it," she said harshly. "After all, it no longer concerns me, does it?"

"No indeed," Stella said quietly. "Glyn is no longer your love. Don't care tuppence, do you?"

Lydia walked to the Howe's house and called out as she walked in. Only Tomos was there, sitting in the small office beside the telephones.

"Hello, Lydia, love. How's the business going?"

"Fine, Tomos. I called to see Glyn, is he here?"

"No, won't I do? Better looking I am," he joked.

"I found this wallet when I was tidying up. It's Glyn's so I thought I'd better bring it straight round in case he's worried about it."

"No need to rush. I doubt there's any money in it."

"I . . . we didn't look, only to see if there was a name," she said.

"Stay for a cuppa, he'll be back soon."

She couldn't stay. Suddenly embarrassed about her intention to tell Glyn she knew about his money, she realised with a jolt that she was interfering, Glyn's business was no longer hers. Still tender from the way he had hurt her, for a while she had forgotten, acting as if they had merely quarrelled and would one day soon make up and be as they were before. Refusing the offer of a cup of tea, she was anxious to get out of the house. She no longer wanted to see Glyn's face when he realised she knew about the money. Hurrying out of the house that had always been like a second home, she ran with her head down, hoping she wouldn't bump into Glyn and have to explain.

On Monday afternoon Molly called at the newly opened wool shop after a visit to the police station on behalf of Mr and Mrs Frank.

"They're a bit upset," Molly whispered as Stella and Annie were not far away, in the back room. "Those medals and a few pieces of valuable jewellery which had been stolen from Mr and Mrs Frank are being returned," she reported.

"Aren't they pleased?"

"No, it brings it all back, see. The burglary while they were in bed fast asleep. Finding the medals and jewellery and money missing. It reminds them of how vulnerable they are, him being partly blind and her so deaf."

"But the medals, Mr Frank must be glad to have them back in the family?"

"What family? There's only those two and a couple of distant cousins several times removed or whatever. No, they don't want them back. Refusing to accept them they are. That's why I had an afternoon off to go to the police station and sort it out."

"Such a shame. He must have been so proud of them."

"He was. Now they feel uneasy with them in the house," Molly sighed. "Medals won by Mr Frank, and his father and grandfather during famous wars, but he won't even look at them."

"Perhaps he's afraid that if someone wanted them badly enough to break in and steal them sixteen years ago, someone else might have the same idea now?" Lydia suggested.

"That's right! I'd never thought of that. I imagined they'd be overjoyed to get them back but they're going straight to the bank and there they'll stay until they can arrange to sell them. Sad isn't it, what effect a burglary can have? Long after the event it causes misery. Poor dabs, they're ill and practically housebound, and they have to have this to contend with, making them feel unsafe, even in their own home. Pity it is that the stuff was found."

"What's more disturbing is that it must be someone around here. Someone we know. Someone who has waited for years afraid to dig up the cache and sell it, until now." Hesitantly she added, "Someone perhaps, who's so short of money he'll take a chance and go to the castle and recover it."

"Thinking of Glyn again, are we?" Molly asked. "That's ridiculous and you know it! I know you and I toyed with the idea of him being involved but neither of us really believed it. Desperate for money he might be, but digging up there at night and pushing you and me down the slope where we might get hurt? Never! And even when he was a boy, could you see him breaking into houses and taking valued oddments? No, the Howe's are a good, honest family and neither Tomos nor Glyn are the type."

"What 'type' does it take to steal and cheat and frighten people? Criminals don't wear a badge, or have shifty eyes or a cruel mouth, do they?"

"If Glyn had all those plus black and broken teeth I still wouldn't believe he was a thief!" Molly laughed, "and neither would you!"

Lydia told Molly about the ten thousand pounds. "And, he did turn up soon after we heard the dog howling and after Stella and I saw the man running away from the castle that night."

"Fancy going up there and having a look?" Molly asked. "The police have re-sealed the entrance, but Tomos and I – we've found a way in again."

"I don't think so, I—"

"Come on, it'll be a lark. There's no one likely to be about now everything's been found."

"Not everything. There's still money missing."

"Notes that are out of date. No one could spend them unless a bank changes them. Spent years ago they were for sure. Come on, 'Never let it be said your mother reared a jibber'!" she quoted with a laugh.

"I wonder how long that ten thousand has been in Glyn's account?" Lydia frowned. "Could it have been there for sixteen years?"

"Don't talk tripe!"

With Stella keeping an eye on the shop, the two girls collected a couple of torches, and put on heavy raincoats. They were laughing as they walked along the lane leading to the quarry, and clambered up the steep slope and over the fence into the allotments. The second fence which had been six feet high and intended to keep people from entering the castle grounds, was flattened by regular use to a leaning and battered two feet. They stepped over with ease and walked through the shrubs up to the narrow path which led around the outside of the castle.

Imminent rain in the form of a heavy mist shrouded the view when they reached the castle entrance. From the ancient gateway on the elevated site, the view across the bay towards the pier, normally so breathtaking, was invisible. Only the few shop window lights succeeded in piercing the mist which soon turned into rain.

Pulling up their hoods, Molly led the way around the outer walls to the place where she and Tomos met regularly. Getting into the castle was made easy with the use of a ladder, which Molly and Tomos left hidden among the overgrown nettles, brambles, and the dead and dying wild flowers that in summer added to the beauty of the place.

They walked through the empty rooms and crawled into the almost filled underground room that had been a cellar. Men working for the police had examined the shallow room but it had settled back into its quiet peace. They went into each room and area they passed, taking their time, glancing around with casual indifference. Neither girl admitted they were avoiding going to the old kitchen, where the body of Rosie Hiatt had been found, for as long as possible.

There was no sign of any further activity and Lydia wanted to abandon the visit and return to the warmth and safety of the shop. "What are we looking for?" she said in exasperation. "We shouldn't have come. Let's go back and have a cup of coffee."

"We ought to look at the kitchen, Lydia."

"Why? There's nothing left to find. The police have searched thoroughly and they've got electronic equipment. What do you expect us to see that they missed?" she said irritably. "This was a stupid idea."

The rain, darkening the already dark afternoon, was adding to the gloom of the place and making her uneasy. The walls were wet, dripping rain which made gentle sounds that seemed threatening. The rooms with their shadowed doorways offered shelter to anyone who might be hiding, looking out at them from the blackness. The sensation of eyes watching their every move increased by the minute. Rosie's death was a tragedy and being here, ghoulishly enjoying the atmosphere of danger, was wrong. They had no right to be here.

"Creepy, isn't it?" Molly whispered when she stopped a few inches into the doorway of the barrel-vaulted storeroom. "Come on, we'll have a quick look at the kitchen and then go. I promised to be back to get Mr and Mrs Frank their tea at four."

Along the open corridor, out into the courtyard. Their nervousness increased as they looked towards the imposing gateway a little to their left. In front of them was the old kitchen. To the left of it, between the kitchen and the gateway, stone steps curved up leading to the battlements. Another stairway, left again of the gate, also led upwards, this time under cover. and it was in the doorway to this one that Lydia detected a slight movement. She covered her mouth to stifle a scream and Molly grabbed her arm and looked in the direction her friend was staring.

"What is it, Lydia?" she whispered.

"I don't know. I saw someone, or something, over by there, in the doorway of the spiral staircase," Lydia's voice was choked with fear.

"Come on, it's probably a bird. Dozens of pigeons live here." Only slightly reassured, Lydia followed Molly through the entrance and looked at the soggy grass of the kitchen floor.

The turf had been neatly relaid and there were no visible signs of the place ever being disturbed apart from a few places where mud revealed newly joined turves which had not yet knitted together.

Lydia walked across and showed Molly exactly

where the grave had been found, and talked about the sad discovery for a while, then a movement caught Lydia's eye.

"Molly. I saw it again. There *is* someone in that doorway!" They looked towards the entrance to the stone spiral staircase and this time, Molly saw it too. A small movement, as if someone standing there had moved further inside.

"Let's get out of here!" Molly muttered.

Both girls began to run back to where they had left the ladder and it was as they went through the chapel block that they realised someone was following. Panic stricken, they held hands and crouched as they hurried through the rooms and corridors, up steps, stumbling occasionally in their haste.

In their agitation they took a wrong turning, climbed a dozen steps through a short passageway and found themselves on the roof of a lower room and there was only one way off it, the way they had come.

It was a terrible moment to have to return back down the few steps they had climbed, back to the corridor where they feared someone was waiting for them. Although the rain had darkened the air, it was still daylight. Yet it looked darker still on the stairway, looking from the open air down into the gloom of the building. It was impossible to see if there was anyone in there, he would be lost in the ominous blackness.

Trying not to make a sound, they stepped down the twelve steps, each counting but without knowing why. At the bottom, Molly was leading and she peered around the corner and came face to face with a man.

"Well! Miss Jones and Miss Powell," Detective

Superindendent Richards said. "Perhaps you would like to tell me what you're doing here?"

"Oh, thank goodness it's you!" Lydia gasped.

"What are you looking for?" The voice was harsh, the eyes steely and the policeman who had been so helpful and comforting to Lydia had vanished. The face now glaring at her was no longer kind. "Come on. Tell me what you were doing or we'll go to the station and sort it out there!"

"Nothing. We weren't doing anything. Just – I don't know. Coming in for a bit of a dare I suppose."

"That's all," Molly added urgently. "I dared Lydia to come here."

"It isn't the first time you've been here since the discovery of Rosie Hiatt's body, is it Miss Powell? Not the first, nor the second. Regular meetings, isn't it? With someone's husband. You're a bit like Rosie herself, don't you think?"

"Don't you dare talk to me like that!" Molly stormed. "I'm not a tart!"

"All right. I'm sorry. But I want to know what you were looking for."

"Now listen to me," Molly stormed, fright making her brave. "Getting soaked we are, standing here listening to insults and answering stupid questions! It's pelting down in case you haven't noticed! Come on, Lydia. We're going."

"You'll have to wait until I replace your ladder," Richards said.

"Come on, I've had enough of this." She glared at the policeman and pulling Lydia after her, hurried to the place where they had entered. The ladder was still as they left it, and both girls climbed out while the man watched them, his face cold and disapproving.

"I recommend you both stay away from here,

unless you want to answer a lot of questions," he called after them.

"I've a damned good mind to pull the ladder up after us," Molly shouted back.

"You can if you wish," he replied. "I have a key."

With Lydia's help, Molly hauled up the ladder and threw it down where it was usually hidden.

"I hope he wasn't bluffing," she laughed as they ran through the allotments and down to the road.

When Lydia arrived home that evening, with her father and mother, the taxi was driven by Glyn. He helped her mother up to her bedroom and Billy tucked her in while Glyn ran back down the stairs.

"Thank you for returning my wallet," he said to Lydia who was already washing rice for the evening meal. "How did you know it was mine?" he asked.

She turned, prepared to lie, but instead said, "I looked inside, of course. I saw your name on the bank statement with the balance of thousands of pounds. Does Tomos know? You pestering him for extra work and taking money from his pocket. Does he know?"

"He does now," Glyn said ruefully. "That was careless of me wasn't it? Leaving it for everyone to see?"

"Not everyone. Just Auntie Stella and me, and your brother of course."

"One day I'll explain," he said softly. "If you can wait a while, you'll understand."

"I doubt it," she said sharply. "Now, if you'll excuse me I have to get the meal ready." She pushed him towards the door and closed it firmly behind him.

Superintendent Richards turned up at the shop the following morning. "I want you to come with me,"

161

he said, but he was smiling. The stern, harsh look was gone.

"Am I under arrest, then?" she asked. Her returning smile was wavery. She wondered if something else had happened at the castle and if she and Molly were thought to be implicated.

"Just something I want you to see," he replied.

Leaving Stella once more in charge, the policeman led her along the lane which led past the entrance to the allotments then on to the old quarry. At the allotment gates, he stopped and unlocked them, guiding her to where her father and Gimlet had their plots. He pointed to where a bonfire had been built. Lydia frowned and looked around her.

"See anything you recognise, Miss Jones?" he asked. Lydia shook her head.

Richards didn't offer any further explanation but stood there patiently as if capable of standing there for the rest of the day. Lydia looked at the dereliction of the year's small harvests, and the few green survivors, like chives and parsley, sprouts and winter cabbage. Her father's allotment was furthest away, next to that of Gimlet, and she walked towards it.

Another bonfire had been started, smaller than the first one she had noticed. Thrown across it, half hidden by dead twigs and brown curling leaves was a coat. Curiously she walked towards it. Brown, it was, and not unlike the one belonging to Matthew.

"That jacket," she said. "Matthew Hiatt had one like that, although it's difficult to see properly."

"Had one?"

"Well it was taken from—" Too late she remembered that the incident in which an intruder entered their house had not been reported.

"Go and take a closer look, Miss Jones, before you tell me exactly what happened to the jacket," he said and the steeliness was back in his voice.

She walked forward and picked up the jacket, slipping debris from it onto the garden. She examined the button and saw that it had been recently fixed. "It is Matthew's! I sewed that button on for him," she said, offering it up for him to see. "And that repair on the sleeve, I did that too."

"Anything else you recognise, Miss Jones?" There was something accusing in the way he kept saying 'Miss Jones' and she was anxious then to assure him she had no more secrets. She looked around at the partly dug plot and at the rubbish that had been gathered together for burning. Half hidden by the leaves which a windy day had blown there and a rainy day had flattened into a mulch, was a black woollen hat.

"There's a hat here," she said. "Shall I pull it out?" He didn't reply so she bent down and unearthed it from the litter that concealed it. A pom-pom, a bright green pom-pom showed boldly, cheerfully in the dull light. She frowned, her memory teasing her. She had seen a hat like this, but where? Then she gasped. Memories of the moment she and Glyn had come upon the body of Rosie Hiatt returned as if it had happened moments, not weeks ago.

"I remember seeing one like this the night we found poor Rosie Hiatt," she said in disbelief. "How could I have forgotten? It was on the ground near the garden fork as if it had just fallen from its handle." She turned and stared at him, her eyes wide with alarm. It was so distinctive someone would remember who made it – and for whom. "Was this what someone was afraid I would remember? Remember and tell the police?

The phone calls weren't specific, just warning me to keep my mouth shut." She was talking, not to the policeman, but to herself.

"Phone calls? A knitted hat? Come on, Miss Jones." Richards was smiling again now. "I think you need to tell me all that happened, don't you? And this time, we won't leave anything out. Right?"

They went back to the shop and his first words were to extract a promise that she would not mention the hat to anyone at all. She willingly agreed. Then, while Stella served a surprisingly steady stream of customers, and Annie claimed she was being ignored, Richards took her through everything that had happened. As she talked she had the increasingly alarming sensation that she was placing Glyn firmly in the front of a line of suspects.

Even when she insisted she had never seen him wearing the hat, he went on about Glyn.

"I'm sure it wasn't Glyn who pushed me out of the way that night when the body was found," she insisted as the questioning became closer and closer to an accusation against Glyn. "The man who ran out of the bushes and pushed me down the slope was a heavier man. Taller than Glyn and, although I don't remember even glancing at his face, I'm sure I'd have known if it was Glyn. I've known him all my life," she added.

"And expected to marry him, I hear."

"Yes, well, things change. We grew up together and it was nothing more than that really."

"No bitterness then?"

"Friends we are and nothing more. It took us a long time to realise it, that's all."

"You're still fond of him," he pressed.

"Of course."

"Fond enough to protect him if you thought he might be in trouble?"

"I don't need to protect him against this! Glyn was never in trouble as a boy. He wouldn't have changed that much. Whoever killed Rosie Hiatt, or buried her body after she died, it wasn't Glyn or Tomos."

"What about Matthew? He was a bit of a lad when he was young. You accept that he has changed a great deal."

"I don't remember much about Matthew when he was a boy. I wasn't very old when he went away. But he's a respectable man now, don't you allow for wild children to change and settle down?"

"Oh yes. Tearaways change. Grown men can change too. But only some of them," he added as he stood to leave. "Not all."

When Glyn called to pick up Annie and Lydia the following morning, he was white-faced with anger. Lydia didn't really look at him as she gathered the things she wanted to take to the shop; her knitting and some patterns she had been browsing through the previous evening. Standing at the foot of the stairs, a hand on the banister, she was suddenly aware of his stillness.

"Go on then, go and fetch Mam, she's all ready." She looked at him then and saw the anger in his eyes. "Glyn? What is it?"

"What have you been telling the police about me? Making up stories and giving them the idea that I was involved in burglaries and burying Rosie Hiatt! That Detective Richards believes I killed her when she came upon me as I was hiding stuff I had stolen!"

"I told him about someone coming into the house and stealing Matthew's jacket. But only after they'd

165

found it half hidden on my father's allotment fire. Nothing I said could have given them the idea you were involved. But finding the coat and the hat—" She stopped, seeing from his expression that he was unconvinced. "It was Matthew who seemed to be involved," she said sadly, "and I can't go and talk to him about it because he's gone off walking again and won't be back until Monday."

"Do the police know that he's missing again?"

"He isn't missing. He's staying at a small guest house, and the police have his address. I have it too and I've tried to phone him but he was out."

On the following Friday Matthew returned.

"I couldn't stay away any longer," he said after kissing Lydia with a passion that surprised and delighted her. "I missed you. The solitary walks I've always enjoyed have lost their charm. I kept thinking of two lovely blue eyes smiling at me, and the soft hair I want to run my fingers through, and a slim, stunningly tantalizing body that I want to . . ." he abandoned that sentence with another kiss. "And," he went on softly, "I had to come home."

They went for a meal, after Stella promised to attend to Annie and Billy and stay with them for the evening. Afterwards they went to a cinema, and while the advertisements were shown she returned to the subject they had discussed over the meal; the jacket and the hat found on Gimlet's allotment.

"Glyn's reaction seems to have been that of a guilty man," Matthew said, "shouting at you for doing your duty. Sorry, love, I know he's been an important part of your life since you were a child, but we never really know anyone. Not even those closest to us. His anger about what you were supposed to have told the police is very suspect, on top of the rest."

166

"On top of the rest?" she queried.

"Appearing so conveniently after you'd disturbed someone at the castle, being so desperately in need of cash, and . . . darling, I wasn't going to tell you this, but I saw Glyn coming out of your house one afternoon before the day you found him hiding those medals."

"What?" she gasped.

"I didn't tell anyone. I presumed it was quite innocent and I didn't see the point of him being grilled by your detective friend over nothing. But I think you should be very, very careful and – I know you won't like me saying this, but I think you should stay away from Glyn, and from Molly."

"What has Molly to do with Glyn?"

"You tell me. Look down there."

It took a moment for her eyes to focus but then she saw without doubt that sitting a few rows in front of them, was Glyn and beside him the familiar figure of Molly Powell.

"It probably isn't what it seems," Matthew said turning her face away from them and kissing her. "There'll be a simple explanation."

"It wasn't what it seemed," Glyn said the following morning when he called for Annie. Lydia refused to listen to his explanations.

"It wasn't what it seemed," Molly said and she insisted on Lydia listening to her. "Tomos and I were almost caught by Melanie and, to save her finding out until Tomos is ready to explain properly, well, we pretended it was Glyn I was with and not Tomos. We went to the pictures and made sure Melanie saw us."

"Molly I refuse to—"

167

"I'm sorry, I know you said you wouldn't cover for us, but this was different and we didn't have much time to think of an excuse. Tomos said the first thing to enter his head."

"And Glyn? Didn't he mind?"

"It doesn't matter any more. His girlfriend, this Cath, she's coming down to stay with the Howe's next weekend."

"Then she is real?"

"It seems so."

Lydia had been all but convinced herself that Matthew Hiatt was her future. Glyn was a mistake. A different kind of love which they had outgrown. She and Glyn were childhood sweethearts and they grew up, there was nothing more between them than that.

Then Molly's announcement threw all her thoughts into chaos once more. Knowing she would be meeting Cath, the girl he had chosen to replace her, turned everything upside down. She was jealous with a tearing aching jealousy that made her want to scream and cry. She hated Cath without knowing anything about her, she didn't even know what she looked like. She might be fat, thin, beautiful or downright ugly. She just hated her for loving Glyn and making him love her.

Chapter Nine

The person who had buried Rosie Hiatt, and the thief who had broken into houses and stolen a variety of valuable items, were considered by most to be one and the same. Matthew insisted they were not.

"The police are wasting time looking for the wrong man if they think the thief killed my sister," he told Lydia on their way home from a meal and a drink at a public house on the edge of the seashore. "I want the man who killed Rosie found and I want him found before I have to leave."

"The police don't even seem sure of how she died, or whether she was killed or died in some other way." Richards had told her that evidence on soft tissue would be long gone and there had been no injury to the neck to suggest strangulation, or any other skeletal clues. She said none of this to Matthew, not wanting him to have more mind-pictures to grieve over.

"Without knowing what they are looking for, how can they hope to find the person who buried her?" she argued.

"I know she was killed by someone. I feel it in my bones."

"Even if she were murdered, sixteen years is a long time. His tracks must be well and truly covered by now," Lydia said. "Wouldn't it be best to forget it, accept that she's dead but try to forget where and how?"

"Would you if she were your sister?" he asked. And she had to shake her head and admit she too would want to know all the answers.

"Not for revenge, that would hurt me as much as the guilty person," she said, "I'd be uprooting a man from his life to face prison, and probably ruining the lives of his wife and children who would know nothing of those events. I would want to know why it happened though, as well as who did it."

"They say she was killed because she was a prostitute," Matthew said looking at her for a reaction.

"Perhaps, but the reasons for choosing that life aren't always understood. Earning a living that way doesn't mean she was bad. I couldn't see myself ending up that way, but perhaps I've just been lucky. It could explain her death though," she added softly. "Clients can get violent, it's one of the many hazards of the job."

"Profession," he said cynically. "It's a profession!"

"If she was killed by one of her clients," Lydia said calmly, "we'll never find him."

"Perhaps someone held her down and cut her wrists."

"Matthew, love, accept it as suicide. She must have been distressed beyond belief to end her life so young, but surely that's easier to live with than knowing someone wanted her dead."

"I just want to know," Matthew sighed.

Tomos knew the time had come when he had to make up his mind. He and Glyn were sitting in their parents' living room one Sunday afternoon, waiting

170

for a call to tell them their taxi was needed. The living room was the back room of the house. The front, with its telephones and radio, was their office from which they ran Howe's Taxis.

"I know I love Molly," Tomos told his brother in a whisper, aware of their mother beyond the kitchen door. "I want to be with her all the time."

"Why don't you tell Melanie, then?" Glyn made it sound simple and Tomos tried to explain.

"I feel I'm letting Melanie down. Guilty I suppose, after the pregnancy, the rushed wedding, then losing the baby and feeling trapped. I know that the trap was just as horrifying for her. I owe it to her to at least let her down gently. We decided then to make the best of it and stay here, making a home with Mam and Dad. I remember how miserable I was at the prospect of the years drifting on and pretending I was content. I try to imagine how it must have been for her. Giving up and telling her the marriage is over is hard to do."

"Are you sure it's not because you still feel something for her?"

"No, love and passion didn't even survive until the wedding. She's a pleasant and kindly girl and I can't hurt her."

They sat beside their mother's fire, listening to the bumping sounds of her rolling pin as she made the apple pie for Sunday lunch. Even now with everything available ready-made and people no longer obsessively clinging to the Sunday roast, Mary Howe still carried on in the same way. Roast beef and Yorkshire pudding followed by rice pudding, or roast lamb followed by apple tart. Tomos and Glyn and Melanie had tried to alter her ways, make life easier for her but Mary still continued with the old traditions.

Tomos glanced across to where his wife's knitting

171

sat abandoned on a chair. "Melanie was never given a chance to try and do things in a style of her own. She's been swallowed up in the routine of the Howe family, hasn't she? And I've allowed it to happen. No wonder Melanie visits her mother so often. She has to escape from the cloying sameness of her life here with us."

"You should have bought a house and started to build your own home," Glyn said. "You might have made a decent life together in a place of your own."

"I know, but the conditions surrounding our marriage made a false start inevitable, and gradually we came to accept the situation without attempting to change it. Perhaps," he added thoughtfully, "neither of us were sufficiently interested."

"What's that she's knitting?" Glyn asked. "Something to sell at Lydia's shop?"

Tomos glanced at the dark blue knitting with little interest. "Probably a sweater for my Christmas present," he said. "I heard her telling Mam that I take so little notice of what she's doing, she can knit something for me, without bothering hiding it when I appear, and know it will be a complete surprise when she gives it to me!"

"Dull and boring, that's you, boy," Glyn smiled.

"If I believed Melanie thought that, I'd tell her I was leaving her today!"

The bang as the oven door closed heralded the entrance of their mother and they sat back in their chairs, like two conspirators caught discussing secrets of the realm.

"What you two up to then?" Mary asked. "If you've nothing better to do, you can set the table for dinner. Your father will be back soon from the allotment and Melanie will be home in a while."

"Where's she gone?" Tomos asked.

"Cardiff to see her Mam and Dad, but she'll be here in time for dinner." Mary's one concession to progress was to have dinner in the evenings and not at midday.

When Melanie returned, Tomos knew there was something on her mind. The cheerfulness was there but forced as if she were holding back a secret worry.

"Mam and Dad all right, love?" Tomos asked.

"They're fine. Asked after you and hoped you'll come with me to see them soon," she replied, the words artificial, rehearsed.

Melanie was subdued during the meal, and although Tomos felt her gaze on him on several occasions, she turned aside when he looked her way. Something was troubling her but he couldn't decide whether it was making her angry, or just excited. He prayed silently, asking that it wasn't a bombshell like her wanting to buy a house, have a child, or rebuild their marriage.

As soon as they had finished, Melanie stood up, volunteering to see to the dishes. Tomos followed her, closing the door behind them leaving Gimlet, Mary and Glyn sitting over coffee. "Now, Melanie," he asked, "what is it?"

"I think you know." She rubbed the plate she was holding with unnecessary force.

"I don't know what you're thinking, do I? Not that clever, although I can see something is bothering you. Your Mam and Dad upset you have they?"

"No. It's nothing to do with them, it concerns you and me. Come on, Tomos, don't pretend you don't know what I'm talking about!"

He felt like he'd been kicked. She knew. She must

173

have found out about him and Molly. Oh, damnation! Why hadn't he told her before this happened? Guilt made his voice harsh as he said, "Time we talked properly, isn't it?" he said. "Melanie, I'm so angry that—"

"No point in being angry, Tomos," she interrupted sharply. "It's happened and nothing will change it."

"You'll leave me, then?"

"I'm leaving you now, tonight, after I've dried the last dish."

"But shouldn't we talk?"

"Since when have we solved anything by talking? Always leaving it until tomorrow, that's your way of dealing with anything, leaving it till tomorrow!"

"I did mean to talk to you. I've tried time and again, but the moment was never right."

"You knew then? About me and Geoffrey?"

Tomos stared at her. "You and . . . Geoffrey? Who is Geoffrey?"

It was Melanie's turn to stare. "Geoffrey is the man I'm leaving you for. You mean you hadn't guessed? Then what were you talking about?"

"I think we should start again," Tomos said throwing down the dish mop and sitting down. "I knew there was someone, all those visits to your parents," he lied. "Tell me everything, about you and Geoffrey. Start at the beginning."

Tomos felt quite light-headed. This was a way of keeping Molly out of the divorce. Perhaps this Geoffrey had given him a chance to bow out of this farce of a marriage gracefully and even with a bit of sympathy.

His feeling of elation stayed with him as he took two lots of revellers to Sunday night parties and he was still bubbling with excitement when a third call was made.

"You can take this one," he said to Glyn as he picked up the receiver. "I have to talk to Melanie."

"Late for that isn't it?" Glyn said cynically, having been told of the strange turn of events.

"Fair play, I want to help her pack, see what she needs now and what she wants me to send on later. And make sure she has enough money and all that," Tomos said. "I don't feel proud of the way this has ended, you know. But," he added with an irresistible grin, "I can't help thanking my lucky, lucky stars!"

The call was from Molly. Glyn offered the receiver back to his brother. "It's Molly," he mouthed.

"Oh, I'd better not talk to her now," Tomos whispered back.

Glyn spoke then listened again. "It's Mr Frank," he explained. "He's fallen and she wants you to go and stay with Mrs Frank while she goes with him to hospital. Go on. I'll see that Melanie gets her cases packed and make sure she doesn't leave before you get back. Right?"

Without further words, Tomos hurried to the cottage where Molly lived with the Franks.

Molly was scarcely holding back tears when Tomos arrived at the front door where she stood waiting for the ambulance. There was time for no more than a few words before the medics were gently taking the half-conscious man out to the ambulance; soothing Mrs Frank and Molly, asking questions, acquiring information, dealing with the patient with a haste that was disguised by their capable and calm efficiency.

Before the ambulance doors closed behind Molly's stricken face, Tomos had no time to say more than, "Molly, love, Melanie is leaving me. It's going to be all right." He wasn't sure she had heard.

He helped Mrs Frank back up to her bedroom,

175

where she had been sitting in an armchair reading, and made her a fresh pot of tea. She was trying so hard to be brave but Tomos could see she was trying tensely to hold back tears. He went to the door of her room and said, "Just down the stairs I'll be. You only have to call and I'm there." He went down the stairs whistling cheerfully and made a few noises so she wouldn't think he was down there listening. He hoped that a few tears would release the tension for her.

He waited for half an hour popping up at intervals to make sure Mrs Frank was all right, then, after ringing the hospital and being told Mr Frank was being examined by a surgeon, he returned to Mrs Frank's room.

"No news, yet," he said. "The hospital said to ring in an hour, but I expect Molly will ring you before then."

"Thank you." Mrs Frank spoke calmly and Tomos hesitated. She looked so controlled, the skin on her pale face paper-thin, her eyes heavy with the after effect of tears. Should he stay or leave her on her own?

"I'm perfectly all right if you'd rather go down and watch television or something," she said.

Hearing in the formal words the underlying plea for him to stay, he grinned and said, "Well, if you're sure you don't mind, I'd rather stay here with you. Lonely it is down by there."

"Then you can bring another cup of tea and sit here with me to drink it."

"A pleasure," he said but inwardly he chuckled. Always a formidable woman, age hadn't changed her that much. Molly had often told him how Mrs Frank ordered her about in a style that went out of fashion

176

fifty years before, and how she accepted it with good humour knowing the kindness that hid behind the brisk formality.

Taking the tea tray and even adding an embroidered cloth which he found on a side table, he returned to Mrs Frank, quirked an eyebrow questioningly and lifted the teapot. On her regal nod, he poured tea into the eggshell-thin cups.

This was, he thought with a sense of affection for the old lady, rather like Mrs Havisham and Pip in *Great Expectations*, only without cobwebs and dust. The old lady and her house were spotless enough even for his Mam to approve. But the atmosphere and the mannerly behaviour created a time-warp in which he had returned to the gentility of life before the last war. He used the small silver tongs and added one lump of sugar to her tea and handed it to her, thinking the experience was far from unpleasant.

"What are you going to do about Molly?" Mrs Frank demanded, almost making him spill his tea. "Isn't it about time you made up your mind?" She stared at him with shrewd and piercing eyes, which were as blue as the pattern on the cup, and hostile.

"I – well, yes." he spluttered. Then he told her about the shock of having Melanie telling him about her affair before he could explain about his own. To his relief she laughed and the slight tension between them eased.

"I think Molly hoped you and Mr Frank didn't know," he said. "She loves you very much and didn't want to cause you worry."

"We love her too and loving her doesn't mean making her so much our servant she doesn't have a life of her own. If we live to be a hundred – and we'll certainly try – we don't want her to be left without anyone who cares."

"I care, but it's been difficult, I haven't wanted to hurt Melanie any more than she's been hurt already. Now it's different, and our future, mine and Molly's, depends at least partly on you. She won't have you distressed in any way and she won't leave you, whatever we decide. You do believe that, don't you?"

"Of course."

A phone call from the hospital assured them that no bones had been broken but they were keeping Mr Frank in for a few days for rest and to be sure he was over the shock of the fall. Molly stayed all night at the hospital and Tomos stayed with Mrs Frank.

Lydia and Matthew continued to spend a lot of time together, mainly thanks to the assistance of Stella.

"Sometimes I feel I don't live at home any more," Stella said, laughing as Lydia prepared to leave her mother in Stella's capable care and meet Matthew. "The days I'm home I help you in the shop, and my evenings are spent here, looking after Annie and getting a bit of supper for your dad."

"Do you mind?" Lydia asked as she was about to put on her coat. "We could stay in tonight if you want to go home?"

"No I don't mind, love. It's time you had a bit of fun and," she glanced at Lydia, frowning slightly and added, "it won't be for much longer, will it? Christmas will soon be upon us and after that, well, what are Matthew's plans? Has he said?"

"No, and I haven't asked. Just enjoy it while I can, that's what Molly advises."

"Different for her now though, isn't it?"

"Is it? I haven't seen her for a few days. Not travelling to work together every day like we used to, we lose touch."

Stella told her the previous day's events, about the surprise of Melanie leaving Tomos, and Mr Frank's fall and about Mrs Frank accepting Tomos and Molly's relationship. "So, things are working out for Molly and I expect she'll recommend something different from 'live for today' now." She touched her niece's shoulder affectionately. "Don't depend on things working out so well for you and Matthew, love. I don't think he's the type to offer you a firm commitment, not like Tomos who's a home-bird at heart. They both are; Tomos and Glyn."

"This mysterious 'Cath' is supposed to be coming here this week, so we'll all be able to have a look at her at last." Lydia spoke light-heartedly but the ache of Glyn leaving her hadn't lessened. Even when she was with Matthew she felt only part of her was involved.

"Been invited to meet her, have you, then?" Stella queried.

"I've never needed an invitation to go to the Howe's. Why should anything be different now?"

"It is different though, isn't it?" Stella said. "You still feel something for Glyn."

"Matthew is much more romantic and generous and fun. No, I don't feel anything for Glyn, except as a childhood friend."

"I loved someone else as you know, before I married your uncle Sam."

"Yes, you told me. But you loved Uncle Sam best, didn't you?"

"I never stopped loving the first one and I always regret putting pride before common sense and refusing him after a . . . Well, he let me down, went out with someone else. I should have forgiven him. My life would have been completely different if I'd been sensible then."

"But it isn't like that with Glyn and me. He found someone he loved more."

"And if he changed his mind, would you forgive him? I didn't, and I've regretted it."

"I can't see that situation arising, can you? Cath is coming to meet his family and they'll probably discuss wedding plans and—" Her face broke up with misery as she mumbled almost inaudibly "Oh, Auntie Stella, I want to run away." She turned to her aunt to be hugged.

"I know, my lovely girl. But don't show him how you feel. Pride definitely helps at moments like these, when you want to be brave."

News that Cath had arrived and that she had brought someone with her, reached Lydia via Molly.

"It was Tomos who met them at the station and brought them out," she told Lydia the following evening. "Won't say a word, mind, irritating man that he is. He says Glyn wants you to meet her without any preconceived ideas, whatever that might mean!" Molly was taking the opportunity of a brief visit to see Lydia's new shop while Mrs Frank was being taken by Tomos to visit Mr Frank in hospital.

She didn't stay long and left Lydia puzzling over Glyn's girlfriend, Cath, and the prospect of being introduced. "I can't promise to be civil, mind!" she called after a laughing Molly.

Christmas was fast approaching and the small shop was becoming very busy. Small gifts wrapped in glittery paper or cellophane to add to their appeal were piled into the small bow window and every evening the displays were replenished and changed as items sold out and new ones arrived.

With only two weeks to go, Lydia took out the contents and did a very special display. Covering boxes and adding tinsel to the edges, crepe paper folded and stretched, and lengths of silver tinsel made the window a spectacle to attract the eyes of every passer-by. News spread about the display and the contents, and the shop was busier still. Every evening Lydia and Stella sighed and collapsed into a chair when the door finally closed.

"If this goes on we'll be making a fortune!" Lydia gasped.

"But it won't, love," Stella warned. "Once Christmas is over, things will settle down to a quiet, steady pace. Not too quiet I hope," she added. "I'd miss all this now. I've enjoyed it more than I'd imagined, haven't you?"

"It's succeeded in taking my mind off Cath!"

"You haven't seen her yet?"

"No. And I won't let Dad or Molly talk about her either. The sooner Glyn takes her back to London the better."

"I've met her," Stella said.

"Lucky old you! Don't tell me she's pleasant, or pretty or clever or – whatever. I don't want to know. Right?"

"Right."

Refusing to talk about Cath didn't really help. She was so stubborn, she refused to ask even a basic question about her, but Lydia did nevertheless wonder what the woman who had usurped her in Glyn's affection looked like, and hoped they would meet before the woman left again for London, "Even if only to settle my curiosity and have a face to dislike," she told Stella.

"Why don't you come with me tonight and meet her?" Molly said later that evening when she and Tomos called with Gimlet. "We're having a bit of a family conference and if you come it will take some of the limelight off me!" she admitted. "Gimlet is all right about me and Tomos getting together but Mary, well, you know what a traditionalist she is, she thinks Tomos should be trying to get Melanie back, not making plans with me."

"Sorry, Molly, I can't."

"Going out with Matthew Hiatt? Bring him as well, the more the better I'd be pleased."

"No it isn't that. I couldn't walk through that door and wait to be introduced to Glyn's new girlfriend, you can understand that can't you?"

"Not so much of the girl, mind," Molly whispered. "Older than him she looks to me."

"I don't want to know!" Lydia was adamant. A few days later she had no choice but to be introduced to Catherine Wesson.

Walking down the lane towards the wool shop, she was carrying bread and a few items for their evening meal when a taxi pulled up and Glyn stepped out. He called her but she pretended to misunderstand and waved casually and quickly entered the shop. She didn't want to talk to him and have to refuse an invitation to meet this Cath who was older than him but whom he had chosen instead of her! A few minutes later he followed her in.

Stella came out expecting to see a customer and when she saw Glyn and the woman with him she greeted them politely then backed out and called Lydia.

Lydia walked into the shop with her smile in place, ready to serve a customer and the smile stiffened but didn't quite fade when she saw Glyn. Her gaze fluttered between him and the woman standing beside him; a tall, rather plump woman, dressed against the damp, cold weather. Her hair was hidden by a tightly fastened head-scarf, emphasising the heavy-jowled face. But brown eyes greeted her warmly with a generous smile. Glyn began to speak but the woman interupted him.

"Hello," she said stepping forward and offering a hand. "I'm Catherine Wesson, and you are – Lydia? What a lovely name," she said as she took Lydia's hand in both of hers in a way that made Lydia warm towards her. The smile relaxed and Lydia, said, "I'm sorry I haven't been down to see you, Tomos and Molly said you'd like me to, but the shop, garments to finish, and with Christmas coming and—"

"Don't worry, but I do want us to talk. Perhaps you'll come soon and we can get to know a little about each other? What about tonight?"

There seemed no way of refusing without being ungracious and somehow, now she had met Catherine Wesson, that wasn't appropriate.

Setting off that evening to meet Cath, Lydia congratulated herself in the grown-up way she was handling herself. But she admitted, it was more to do with the warmth and gentleness of Cath than her own maturity. There was no way I could be rude to her, she thought to herself. I find it impossible to dislike her.

She was nervous though and, as a sort of safety net, had arranged for Matthew to call for her an hour after the time she planned to arrive.

Cath stood up to greet her and after a few moments

of polite talk, called out, "Come on in, my lovely, come and meet Lydia." Lydia looked expectantly towards the kitchen door wondering who could be there, but who ever she expected it was not this. A small child, about four or five years old, hugging a doll, a rather anxious look in her dark eyes, stepped towards her and said formally, "How d'you do, Lydia? I'm Cath two. Spelt TWO," she added with a smile reminiscent of the older Catherine."

"Your daughter?" Lydia asked and wondered, with a sickening jolt, whether the child was Glyn's.

Catherine laughed. "No, I'm neither married nor a Mum. I'm her aunt." She hugged the little girl affectionately. "Her lovely Mum died, you see, and her Dad is starting a new business to make a home for her, isn't he Cath Two? Until he gets a house, I'm bringing her up. We're learning how to do it together, aren't we my lovely?"

Any unease was dissipated by the entrance of the child. She was a real chatterbox and at once sat on Lydia's lap and began telling her the names of all her dolls of which she seemed to have a great number called Sue. Big Sue, Seaside Sue, Little Sue, Pink Sue, Baby Sue. The list seemed endless.

"Don't you think a different name might make life easier?" Lydia said laughing.

The little girl thought about this solemnly for a while then said, "No. Sue is my favourite name and when I can't think of another Sue I'll call the next one Susan. Then Susanna." Another list threatened and they all laughed. The little girl was obviously happy in the Howe's home and felt easy with them all.

An hour had passed with surprising speed and Lydia listened for the doorbell to herald the arrival of Matthew. Aware that Matthew might not want to come inside, she put on her coat so she would be ready when he called.

"Are you talking about Matthew Hiatt?" Cath asked, when she explained. "Glyn told me he was back in the village. I wonder what he wants?"

Lydia glanced at Glyn who, guessing her thoughts said. "I didn't see any point in telling her. She knew Rosie you see."

"What happened to Rosie? And why *is* Matthew back?" Cath asked, looking from one face to another.

"You know him?" Lydia asked in surprise. "I thought you lived in London?"

"I do, but I was born here. I moved away when my father was transferred to Tottenham, years ago. I remember Matthew very well. Who wouldn't? A right tearaway he was. And I lived next door to his sister, Rosie," she went on. "Disappeared didn't she? Off with some man in search of a better life and who's to blame her?"

"Go into the kitchen and fetch me some more cakes will you my lovely?" Mary asked the little girl. When she was out of the room, Glyn told Cath about the body being found.

"Buried up at the castle! But what on earth happened? How did she die?"

They answered her questions as well as they were able. But it was clearly a great shock to her.

"Reading about a possible murder in the papers, and seeing it on television is one thing. When it's someone you know, it, well, it makes it much more frightening. Murder doesn't touch many lives in spite of all the numbers of deaths that occur. I can't believe it. Was it one of her clients d'you think?"

Glyn thought of his father and Billy Jones being

involved with the young woman and muttered uneasily that it seemed the most likely possibility.

"I remember the day she left very well," Cath said. "There was always plenty of gossip about the Hiatts. Rosie had a room with Mrs Harry, didn't she? After you and Mary had taken her in for a while."

"Poor Matthew. He was very upset coming home a few weeks ago to try and find out where she'd gone, and then being told she was dead," Lydia said.

"Matthew wasn't that worried about her at the time. He had too many worries of his own," Cath said quietly. "Into every illegal way of making money that boy was, and he cleared out just ahead of the police, who suspected him of a series of burglaries. Lots of things disappeared at that time, including my father's shotgun. Remember, Glyn?"

"Whatever he was like then, he was horrified at learning that his sister was dead and possibly murdered." Lydia spoke sharply. "How could you not understand the horror of being told that?"

"Sorry. I didn't mean to sound so heartless. Of course it must have been a shock. Thinking back, I forgot for a moment. It's a shock for me too. I was talking to her only hours before she was reported missing. Not that the police took her disappearance seriously. They thought, like most of us, that she'd gone off with some manfriend and would turn up again when he – or she – got bored."

Lydia was right in thinking Matthew didn't want to come in and she was thankful he didn't. Cath's reminiscences might have distressed him. But her mind was filled with doubts. Everyone said Matthew had been a problem, but a gun? She remembered that the police had found an oilskin near Rosie's body which they said had been used to wrap a gun. Could he have been involved in more than the wildness of youth?

On the way home she told him what Cath had said and questioned him.

"Lydia, I have to trust you. I love you and if you love me you have to promise never to repeat what I'm going to tell you."

"Short of murder, I promise," she replied, giving a quivering smile.

"Rosie's death was one hell of a shock. You have to believe that. I had no idea she wasn't living, acting in her usual happy-go-lucky way and getting plenty of fun from life. I even imagined her married and settled down with a husband, kids and a mortgage. But dead? Possibly murdered? It's nightmare stuff."

"But the gun? That was something to do with you?" she asked when a silence stretched out.

"That was something to do with me," he admitted. "I'd robbed several houses. Yes, including that of Mr and Mrs Frank. Spite that one, really. He was always chasing me off the pavement, telling me to keep away from respectable people and twice he hit me for climbing into his precious garden to retrieve my ball. It was no use to me, the stuff I took from the Frank's. I usually looked for money. Where Cath Wesson lived there was a weak back door and I used to go inside and eat some food from the larder, imagining how they'd puzzle over what happened to it. I was just a kid," he said and she smiled, seeing in her mind that unhappy, undisciplined, defiant little boy.

"Then one day I found the gun. Mr Weston had been shooting and had left it out to clean. A box of cartridges had been carelessly left too, a box half full, and I whipped the lot."

"What did you do with it?" Lydia asked, dreading

to hear the answer, wondering if she'd be able to keep her promise.

"I buried it up in the castle with the stuff I'd taken and couldn't sell."

It took a moment to sink in, then she whispered, "It was you who was digging in the old kitchen?"

"It was me."

"And you who found—? Oh, Matthew, what an awful experience, finding Rosie like that."

The memory of that awful moment choked him and for a moment he couldn't go on. "I was searching for the gun and the boxes of stuff I'd stolen, thinking that if the castle was being repaired the workmen might find them. Then, when I thought I'd found it, I saw." He stopped and took a few deep breaths, the horror of it returning. "I thought it was a necklace at first, would you believe that? I wondered if it was part of the stuff I'd buried. Then, then I realised it was a body. I remember running, scrambling through that window, imagining a hundred ghosts chasing after me along the path. Blundering through trees, down the slope, pushing someone aside. It was terrifying."

"You didn't know then that it was your sister?"

"How could I? I didn't believe she was dead. Lydia, I still can't forget the horror of being told it was poor Rosie."

"Of course you can't. Your own sister," she murmured sympathetically.

"No, you don't understand. I hated her you see. I hated her for not bothering to keep in touch with me. I was a criminal and I'd been living on my wits for years but I was only seventeen and I had no one. She promised that whatever happened we'd never lose touch and I hated her for letting me down. All the time she was—"

"Come on in," Lydia said, guiding him like a child. "Stella's there, looking after Mam, but we'll stay down in the kitchen. I think you need to talk and talk until you can get the pictures out of your mind."

Stella and Billy were playing cards but when Lydia explained that she and Matthew needed to talk, they didn't interrupt, just continued with their game of rummy, while Annie slept peacefully above. When Matthew left, Billy walked Stella home without asking any questions.

In the Howe's home, discussions had continued on Matthew and Rosie Hiatt. Cath Two was in bed, Gimlet and Mary went up and still the talk went on. Cath remembered the day Rosie disappeared with surprising clarity. At midnight, when the lights finally went out, Glyn and Tomos and Molly persuaded Cath to talk to the police.

"It was all so long ago," she argued. "How can it help after all this time?"

"How can you tell? What you remember, added to what they already know, might be enough to help them discover what happened the night Rosie Hiatt disappeared.

Cath was unwilling to talk to the police. There was something she hadn't explained to Glyn and Tomos. Her memories of the night Rosie Hiatt disappeared were very clear. She had been taking a short cut through the castle grounds via the allotments. It was almost dark and she had seen men tidying their tools away and closing their tool-sheds, having finished work for the evening. Standing under the trees she had seen Rosie, who was waiting for someone. She remembered clearly the young woman's excited mood.

She told Cath she was pregnant and was laughing, describing how determined she was that someone would pay. From the look on Rosie's face she was going to enjoy the situation in which she believed she had the upper hand.

The following day, the shop was crowded with customers and with those who only came to chat. The decorations were decidedly fragile by this time as display after display had been demolished for the items to be sold. Stock was running low and in between serving, Lydia and Stella were making lists of items they would need to see them through the unexpectedly busy few weeks.

Battling her way to the window to retrieve a jumper someone wanted to buy, Lydia was laughing and joking with a customer when she saw a police car stop outside. A constable came in and asked her to go with him to the police station. Gimlet Howe and her father were under arrest.

Chapter Ten

Any warmth Lydia felt towards Cath dissolved like steam on a window under a cat's lick. Thanks to the information she had given the police, her father and Gimlet were under arrest.

Superintendent Richards called and questioned her with alarming thoroughness. She was edgy and he knew it. The reason for her edginess, besides anxiety about the fate of her father and Gimlet, was because of the information given to her by Matthew; information she had promised to withhold.

For all his smiles and friendliness, this clever man could easily persuade her to tell all. He only needed a slight hint that she was holding back and he'd subtly edge the questioning so she would say more than intended. Then there would be no possibility of keeping anything from him.

It was eleven o'clock, the morning after Billy and Gimlet had been taken in for questioning and the Superintendent had called at the house where Lydia waited for news. Annie had refused to leave her bed and Stella had agreed to look after the shop leaving Lydia to deal with her mother.

For a while the Superintendent talked about the discovery of Rosie's body, making her go over and over what happened, making certain she had omitted nothing, then he asked for a cup of coffee and, with relief, she went down to the kitchen to make it. They sat almost companionably then. He asked about the sweater she was making and whether the central heating was adequate and even asked the names of the plants with which the room was decorated. She felt the stress ease out of her. Perhaps it was over now. Her father would soon be home and all the questioning would be ended. He didn't kill the poor girl, the confessions had revealed the truth. Gimlet had found her dead and with her wrists cut. It was definitely suicide, so a charge of concealing the evidence of a crime by burying the body was sure to be all they faced.

"Do you know where Matthew Hiatt is?" he asked suddenly.

"I think he's at the hotel where he's been staying off and on since October. I expect he'll be here later, I dropped a note in for him late last night, telling him about Dad and Gimlet."

"You're wrong. He's left town. He was on the train out of town at seven o'clock this morning. No matter," he added as she began to argue, "we have an eye on him."

"But why? He's probably gone off on one of his walks. I'm sure he will have let his landlady know where he is. Why the hint of secrecy? Surely he isn't suspected of burying Rosie's body? He was devastated when he knew she'd been found."

"Coincidence, mind, him being here when the body came to light, wasn't it? And did he ever explain why he broke into your house and took his jacket?"

Lydia was confused. The man who had entered the house and locked Annie in her room had been accepted as a dream. But the jacket had been taken, and only Matthew had known it was there.

"And that knitted hat, several people have told us how he had one remarkably similar when he arrived here. Never seen it since that night. Could that be the one which ended up on the bonfire." He allowed a moment to pass then added slowly, "The bonfire on your father's allotment?"

"Matthew didn't kill his sister and he wasn't responsible for burying her either, it *is* just coincidences. They do happen, you know."

"Oh, I accept there are such things, but you'd be surprised at how often they aren't coincidences at all, only someone trying to outwit someone else. Take another coincidence. He's quite skilled at appearing at the right time, isn't he?"

The words flew to and fro until Lydia finally gave Richards the opening he waited for.

"What was he doing up at the castle if it wasn't to find and move the body he had murdered and then buried?"

"He wasn't looking for her!"

"Oh, then what was he looking for? A gun? A box of medals? Some jewellery?"

"I don't know," she blustered.

"Rosie was threatening to tell the police where he was hiding. Did you know that? She was his sister but her evidence might have put him in prison. A long way from being a respected head teacher, an ex-jailbird, don't you think? Worth making an effort to avoid that fate, wouldn't you say?" She knew then that to save Matthew from an accusation of murder, she had to tell the policeman what she knew. It was a relief in a way, she wasn't a person who found it easy to lie.

Besides, her worries about Matthew were less urgent since Billy and Gimlet had been taken into police custody. She was too afraid for their fate to worry about much else. Matthew had only been a part of her life for a matter of weeks and the prospect of seeing Billy in prison dominated every other thought, including her promise to Matthew.

Richards listened silently until she had revealed everything Matthew had told her, then he stood up to leave. Thanking her for the coffee, he ran down the stairs without any more questions or even a discussion on what she had said. Her own questions hung in the air without answers. She was left with a feeling of anti-climax and an overwhelming sense of guilt. She had been so afraid for her father and Gimlet she had let Matthew down.

She sat, staring into space and wondering what was going to happen to them all. She was frightened for Billy and Gimlet, and wondered how this situation would affect Matthew's career. She wondered about Glyn and Cath, and herself and Matthew. It was as if everything important to her had been thrown into a giant mixing bowl and stirred into chaotic confusion.

At five o'clock she decided to go once more to the police station for news of her father, then look for Glyn. Annie was sleeping, having taken a sleeping tablet unnoticed by Lydia. As she left the house, her thoughts were on Glyn. Whatever feelings she had for him, or had once had, they were in this together, with both fathers involved in the police investigation.

Cath opened the door and smilingly told her that Glyn was driving someone to the airport and wouldn't be back for a couple of hours. The little girl stood beside her aunt and Lydia couldn't resist bending down and talking to the attractive, but solemn child. She didn't try to begin a conversation with Cath –

194

the person responsible for the arrest of her father and Gimlet – but left without going inside.

She walked along the road to where the allotments lay below the castle, and worked her way around the narrow roads and lanes to Stella's house and shop.

At the gate to the castle grounds, onto which light flooded from the lit shop window, she paused and looked up at the castle. It was late evening and already dark and, with bright lights behind her, it was almost impossible to make out its shape. Was there something up there that would end this mystery? Something to clear her father and Gimlet from the suspicion of murder?

Turning to enter the shop she stopped. Would the police still be watching the place? It had been a while since they were last seen exploring the ruins and the grounds. But perhaps after the revelations about Matthew their vigil would be reinstated? Searching her mind for a reason to go up there, she remembered seeing some teasels growing on the slope between the path around the outer walls and the end of the allotments. Going up to pick them was not the most brilliant excuse ever invented but it would do.

Stella was busy serving customers, the place was full, customers chattered and demanded and Stella was rushing around trying to please them all looking quite harrassed. Going in through the side door and collecting a torch and a pair of scissors, Lydia excused her abandonment of her aunt with the conviction that she would be no more than ten minutes.

The air was still, a mist had crept in from the sea and was clothing the village that nestled beside it, tucking it in for the night. Coloured lights were hazy, both enlarged and weakened by the damp air. The sound from the busy shopping street reached her and gave her a feeling of isolation and loneliness. Down there were happy people gathering the ingredients for their Christmas celebrations and up here against the be-fogged castle she was on her own, looking for heaven alone knew what, fantasizing about making a discovery that would solve everyone's problems in seconds.

The path around the walls was less frequently used now summer had ended and even Neville Nolan and his gang accepted that the place was out of bounds. Branches stuck out and became hazards as she pushed her way along. Leaving the path she started down to where the allotment fence was no more than an occasional glint of metal. Her speed increased with the sharpness of the slope and she was running before she touched the fence.

This area, where both Molly and she had fallen, was even more overgrown. She forced her way through, foolishly clinging to the plan of cutting the teasels in case she was stopped. They were easily found, taller than even the hedge parsley heads which were now untidy with the last of their seed. She took out the scissors she had brought and cut the thick, thorny stems. They would look nice as a window display if they were sprayed with colour. Apt for a wool shop too. Teasels had been used for carding wool ready for spinning for centuries.

Once picked, she found it difficult to carry them. They were long and awkward, getting in the way as she walked through the overgrown trees and the brittle stalks of dead wild flowers. The stems hurt her hands and a handkerchief wrapped around them didn't help. She needed two hands to climb back up the bank too, and seeing her path with only the thin beam of a torch made it almost impossible. She left them where she would find them on her return and began to clamber up the slope on all fours.

She almost turned back then. What was she looking for? And how could she hope to find anything with only a small torch? She realised she was back at the place where she had fallen. The ground was disturbed and great channels showed where her feet had failed to find purchase. Bending again into a crawl she began to climb up to the castle's periphery path.

The earth was insecure, the plants growing there were brittle and had shallow roots which didn't hold the earth. Even under the hawthorns the soil was friable and loose. She had climbed about half way up, only a matter of three feet, when her foot began to slide and she couldn't stop herself slithering slowly, but inexorably, back down. Scrabbling around frantically for something to grip to save her falling, her hands grasped a small object and as her feet slid at an increasing rate at the same moment, she still held it when she landed in an undignified heap near the allotment fence.

She was angry with herself. What a stupid idea this had been. Better off she'd be, going back and helping her aunt serve in the shop. She struggled back to where she had left the bunch of teasels, she might as well have something to show for her stupid behaviour. It was then she realised she was still holding the object she had grasped. In the beam of the torch she saw it was a knife. A two-bladed pocket knfe with one blade, rusted and almost unrecognisable, still open. Instinctively she threw it down, then she stared at it down the beam of her torch.

It must belong to one of the boys who frequented the castle. But what if it didn't? What if it had been here for sixteen years, after someone had slit the wrists of Rosie Hiatt?

Holding it distastefully, she carefully wrapped it in the handkerchief she had been using to hold the teasels, then she marked the place where she thought she had found it, and went down towards the gate.

When she walked into the shop, mud-stained and with her hair sticking up and full of flower seeds, Stella laughed then demanded an explanation.

"It's unlikely it has anything to do with Rosie," Lydia said when the shop was cleared and they sat with a cup of tea in Stella's back room. "Not after all these years. No, it was probably dropped last summer by a tourist sharpening a pencil or something equally mundane. So many people wandering about there and dropping things. It could have come from anywhere. If it was anything to do with Rosie wouldn't it have been found at the time? And with Neville Nolan and his gang spending so much time there, it's unlikely that it's been there sixteen years and not been found."

"When Rosie disappeared, no one looked for a weapon, did they?" Stella replied.

"Oh, I'd best throw it away. I've been watching too much television for sure."

"Glyn's been here looking for you," Stella told her. "I didn't know where you were. Said he'd go back and wait for you."

"Look at the time! I must fly! Mam's on her own. All fuss and feathers she'll be if she wakes up and find herself alone. You know how frightened she gets. What have I been thinking about!"

"I'll just see to the till and I'll be down later to see if there's any news of Billy," Stella said as Lydia hurried home.

Glyn was there, talking to Annie, reading her bits

198

from the newspaper. Annie could read perfectly well and didn't even need glasses but she loved to be read to.

"Being spoilt, are you Mam?" Lydia said as she ran into her mother's bedroom and kissed her.

"Where have you been?" Glyn asked seeing her dishevelled appearance. "Are you all right?"

"Yes, I—" she glanced at her mother, who was watching them, and added lightly, "I'll tell you all the news when I've phoned the police again, and made Mam a cup of tea, right?"

"Glyn's been in touch with the solicitor and he thinks Billy and Gimlet will be released in the next hour," Annie told her happily.

In her delight at hearing the news, Lydia forgot herself for a moment, and hugged Glyn. Embarrassed, she pulled away from him and hurried down the stairs. "I'd better get the food on," she said. "Starved he'll be."

Putting a casserole on to heat through, she turned as Glyn followed her down the stairs and asked him what had happened to her father and his.

"It seems that your father had a row with the girl. I gather she was trying to find someone to take responsibility for the baby she was expecting and both of them were likely candidates! Billy pushed her and my father went back later just to see if she was all right and found her with her wrists cut. It was too late to help her and knowing what a field day the papers would have, he buried her and hoped people would presume she'd left town and not look for her – which was exactly what happened."

"I've half suspected that Dad went with other women, but I've never really faced it before. I don't

199

think he does now. I imagine that affair made him lose his nerve."

"He didn't know until a few weeks ago what my father had done for him," Glyn said. "The reason he doesn't look for sex outside the home is because he's returned, in a way, to his first and true love."

"What d'you mean?"

"Stella," he replied succinctly.

So many things became clear then.

It was much later when she remembered the knife. After a brief explanation, she showed it to Glyn.

"The police will have to see this and they'll probably be annoyed to say the least."

"Annoyed? With me? It's nothing to do with me!"

"For moving it," Glyn explained. It's probably nothing to do with Rosie's death but you shouldn't have touched it."

"I didn't know I had it! I slipped and grabbed at handfuls of soil, hoping to catch hold of a tree root or something solid to stop me falling. My hand just tightened on it instinctively. Like a drowning man clutching a straw I suppose."

There was a knock at the door and Lydia swung around to open it, expecting to see her father, but it was Matthew. "Lydia, I've just heard about your father," he said, ignoring the presence of Glyn. "Is everything all right?"

"Yes, thank goodness. He and Gimlet are probably on their way home this minute."

"And I'd better go home and find out what's been going on," Glyn said. He went to pick up the handkerchief in which the rusted knife was resting and Matthew stopped him.

"What's that? Where did you find it?" he demanded.

Lydia explained and told him that Glyn was going to take it to the police station. "Where in the castle grounds?" Matthew asked, and Glyn hovered at the doorway, anxious now to be off to greet his father. "You didn't go inside the castle did you?" he asked anxiously.

"Can I take it now, Lydia? I must go. I want to be there when Dad gets home. Mam'll be upset and—"

"Thank you for telling me about – you know," she spoke with her head bent, not wanting to mention her father's love for her aunt. If Matthew was curious he didn't ask questions.

"You go, Glyn," he said. "I'll take the knife to the police station while Lydia waits here for Billy. I'll go straight away. They'll want to see this as soon as possible." His eyes were filled with tears as he looked at the small knife, convinced, albeit without reason, that it was the weapon which had ended his sister's life.

"I have the superintendent's telephone number. D'you think we should phone him first? After all he *is* in charge of the investigation."

Matthew talked on the phone then told her he had arranged to meet Richards at the station an hour later. "He said we weren't to discuss it with anyone," Matthew said.

"I think they like to keep fresh information to themselves in the hope that someone will trip themselves up," Glyn said.

"He probably still suspects me," Matthew said ruefully.

Glyn hurried off to welcome his father home, but before Matthew also left, to deliver the knife to

201

Superintendent Richards, Lydia told him that she had betrayed his trust and told the sergeant what he had confided to her. She expected him to be angry but his shoulders drooped and he said quietly, "Perhaps it's just as well. It would all have come out anyway. Finding Rosie's body was bad luck so far as my secret hoard was concerned, but, d'you know, I'm glad it's all out in the open."

"But your career. You might have trouble with the new position. A criminal, even if thoroughly reformed, isn't a popular choice for a head teacher."

"I'll start again, with something new if necessary. Difficult, but not impossible. My army record was a good one."

"I'm sorry, Matthew."

"Don't be." He took her in his arms and held her close. "Another plus might be my starting again here, with you to help me. Does that appeal to you as much as it does to me, Lydia?"

She kissed him but didn't reply. The recent brief hug she had shared with Glyn had created a far greater emotion.

The weather had turned very cold and for several days the radio had been debating the possibility of snow for Christmas and when Billy arrived, the snow came with him. As the door burst open, Billy appeared in a flurry of large snowflakes. He was hugging himself and began talking almost before the door opened, about the perishing weather, enforced idleness, rotten food, the smelly accommodation and the sarcasm of the coppers, "And how," he asked, almost without taking a breath, "is Annie?"

Matthew smiled at Lydia and whispered, "He

seems unharmed by the experience, but I bet he and Gimlet have got a giant of a thirst!" He picked up the cloth and the rusty knife without Billy seeing it, and went out.

When he returned about half an hour later, his coat was patchily white, his face ruddy, his hair edged with fine flakes as if he were a part of the seasonal decorations. Stella had arrived, Billy was sitting in front of a huge fire, Annie had been carried down and was sitting opposite him and Lydia was attending to the three of them as if they were all invalids.

Avoiding being heard by her parents, Matthew told Lydia he had given the knife to the superintendent, who would be calling to talk to her about her discovery later that evening. "If he can get through," he added. "The forecast is for heavy snow and drifts continuing all night and you know how that changes people's plans!"

"I hope he doesn't make it. I don't think I want to see a policeman again for a while," Lydia sighed.

"Do you want me to stay?" he asked.

Lydia shook her head. "No it's all right. Dad will be here. I don't think he'll be going far from home tonight."

Gimlet and Billy were both in need of some *maldod* – some tender loving care – but, after an hour or two of telling their families about their ordeal, they both needed a drink as Matthew had predicted.

Gimlet arrived with Glyn and Tomos and Molly and they took Billy to The Pirate to celebrate with their friends. Stella was taken home by Glyn about nine and when Annie had been put to bed, Lydia decided that Richards must have changed his mind and she prepared to have a bath and go to bed herself. It had been a distressing day.

Glyn joined his father and Billy and the others at The Pirate, but he was uneasy. The pre-Christmas joviality had infected the regular clientele and laughter filled the room, emanating from the various groups. Decorations glittered around the lights and brass shone, reflecting the fire in the huge grate, but Glyn seemed unaware of it all. He was edgy, unhappy, but couldn't explain why. Something rankled in the back of his mind and he couldn't clear his thoughts sufficiently to understand what it was. Leaving the rest of the celebratory party in The Pirate, he went to the police station and asked for Detective Superintendent Richards.

He was told that Richards was not on duty that day and would probably be at home.

"I saw him up at the castle earlier today, mind," one of the constables told him, "but he won't be there now, not in this weather."

"You'll have a note of Matthew Hiatt coming in and handing in a knife found at the castle?" Glyn said. "He was here then."

The two constables looked at the book and at each other and frowned. "There's nothing down here about Matthew Hiatt calling, no mention of a knife being handed in, and the Super definitely hasn't been here today."

Glyn left, his deep, tantalizing thoughts crystallising and adding to his anxiety. Matthew had been lying.

The snow had worsened and the streets were already covered with a couple of inches of snow. The cars passing along the road were making that unmistakable shushing sound as the wheels turned the white to a slushy drab brown, which changed colour where streetlights gave it an orange glow. Glyn felt it seeping into the unsuitable shoes he wore and wished he had thought to wear wellingtons.

What had Matthew done with the knife if he hadn't handed it in? Could he have met Richards somewhere other than the police station? He had telephoned him first. Although, they had only heard Matthew's end of the conversation. What if he had only pretended to talk to the man?

Where was Matthew now? If he hadn't reported the find then what else was he hiding? He pulled his collar up higher and, ignoring the comfort offered by The Pirate's bright windows, he returned to Lydia's house.

The bath was running and the scent of expensive bath foam filled the steamy air. Lydia was removing her clothes when she heard a knock on the door. Probably someone to ask about Billy, she thought with a sigh. Putting her trousers and sweater back on, she ran down the two flights and opened the door. It was Superintendent Richards.

"Oh, I forgot you were coming," she said. "Come in quick before all the heat goes from the house!" The snow swirled in the air. "The weather forecasters are probably right, this looks set to continue all night," she added shivering dramatically.

"I want you to come with me," he said, tight-lipped.

"What, in this? At this time of night? Why, what's happened?"

"It's about the knife you found. You must show me exactly where it was found. It's very important."

"Won't tomorrow do? Nothing will change in

205

this weather. I doubt if even a fox will venture out in this!"

"It could clear your father completely if what you tell me ties in with what we already know about Rosie's death."

"I'll have to stay until Dad gets back. Mam doesn't like being left alone at night."

"We won't be long. Twenty minutes at the most. I don't want your father to know where we're going. I want him completely ignorant of this or he could be suspected of interfering and that would put him in a bad light. On his answers to my next lot of questions, his freedom might depend. Matthew's too. We don't want people saying they'd spoken to you and compared stories, do we? Hurry, we'll be back before ten and I doubt if he'll be home before then."

There was something frightening in the man's demeanour and without further argument, Lydia found wellingtons and coat and followed him. Out of the house, down the steps to the seafront where street lights shone weakly through the polka-dot air, and the sea beyond was invisible.

Without a word he took her arm and hurried her towards the path beside the sea. He walked so fast and held her so tightly, she began to feel she was under arrest. A joke to that effect gained no response. His face looked closed up, unfriendly and steely cold.

Walking around behind the houses and up through the wood towards the castle was difficult as he refused to show a light and there was no lessening of the pace he set. "Why are we going this way?" she demanded.

"I have my reasons, just hurry, will you?"

She was half dragged when she stumbled or when trees pulled at her clothes and she began to feel very frightened. What was he taking her to see? Not another body? Please not, she prayed. She couldn't cope with another shocking sight like Rosie Hiatt. What could he have found up here? And how could he hope to show it to her with with every piece of open ground covered with snow?

She tried to free herself from his grasp, pleading for him to stop, insisting she was out of breath, needed a rest, her face was scratched, her feet were sliding, she couldn't see where she was walking, and couldn't he slow down? All to no avail. He pulled her inexorably up through the steep woodland, half dragged her up the steep slope of the castle mound made slippery by the fresh snow. Around the grounds they went, hugging the hedges until the castle loomed up in front of them through the shower-curtain of snowflakes.

The ladders were in place and there at last, below the window so many people had used for access, he finally stopped.

"Climb up," he said, still holding her arm. "Go on, climb up if you want to save your father."

"I didn't find the knife inside the castle," she tried to explain. "It was further on, below this path."

"Do as I say."

"But why are we going inside?"

"I have something you must see." He forced her to climb up through the window and down the other side.

"It wasn't in here!" she insisted time and again. "I found the knife outside. On the slope below the path." She tried refusing to go any further, but he used force and threats and she had no alternative but to go where he led.

*　　*　　*

Glyn walked back to Lydia's house. The door was unlocked and he went in, calling her name. The scent of bath foam was in the air and he smiled and sat down, waiting for her to emerge from the bathroom. After a while he realised there were no sounds coming from upstairs and he climbed the stairs, walked past Annie's room and saw that the bathroom door was open. Calling her name he pushed it and discovered it was empty, the half-filled bath was still. Lydia's abandoned dressing gown and nightdress neatly placed on the towel rail. Panic beginning to fill him, he went to her bedroom and found that undisturbed.

Searching the house he saw Annie was fast asleep, a book fallen from her hands. Apart from her, the place was deserted. Matthew! She must have gone somewhere with Matthew. He closed the door behind him, slithered his way down the stone steps and hurried to Matthew's hotel. Matthew was reading in his room.

"I left her more than an hour ago," he told Glyn. "I did offer to stay for when that policeman called but she said she'd be all right, with Billy there and the rest."

"We all went out and now there's no sign of her."

They went once again to the police station where they were assured that Lydia had not been brought in and, no, there was no mistake. The Superintendent was definitely not on duty.

"And you still say you have no record of Matthew Hiatt bringing in a knife found by Miss Lydia Jones?" Glyn asked, looking at Matthew as he spoke.

"No record?" Matthew frowned. "I met Superintendent Richards here this evening. He was waiting for me at the corner of the road, said he was on his way here. He took it, thanked me and told me to tell no one. I was asked to instruct Miss Jones to stay in as he'd be calling to interview her later this evening."

The constables could shed no further light on the puzzle and Matthew and Glyn decided they would go and find the sergeant to see if he were able to tell them where Lydia might be.

He lived not far from Stella so it was to Stella they went first, in case Lydia had told her of some plan to go out.

Stella looked up at the castle and shivered. "She wouldn't be up there, would she? Not in this?"

"No," Glyn laughed. "Curious she might be, but she wouldn't go up there on a night like this. Especially not alone."

"She did look upon it as *her* mystery, mind. She might conceivably want to investigate something and go on impulse. She can be stubborn," Stella added, "follows her father in that. If something occurred to her, she might well go up there, even in weather like this."

Matthew went to see if there were any footprints leading up from the gate, but if there had been any, the snow had filled them.

"There were two people walking along the lane behind Mary and Gimlet's house when I was there earlier," Stella said. "Heading for the castle or the wood below it. There's no stopping some courting couples, is there?" She tutted.

"Did you see who they were?"

"In this? No chance! But I remember thinking it looked like a man and a woman, arm in arm they looked to be."

"It was them. I know it was them!" Glyn said.

Gathering torches, Glyn and Matthew jumped the gate and went at a slippery run up the slope towards the castle. Stella telephoned the police, thankful that Lydia had insisted on having her telephone re-installed when they opened the shop.

Forcing her to walk beside him, Richards led Lydia to where they looked at the gateway from inside the ruined building. He twisted her hands behind her and fastened them before she was aware of what he was doing. Then as she threatened to scream, he tied a scarf tightly across her mouth so it bit painfully into her mouth. She tried to get away but he held her almost playfully, pushing and pulling her to the broken walls of the kitchen. There, in almost the exact place where Rosie had been found, was a grave.

He held her almost like a lover, pressing her against him and looking down into her wide, terrified eyes. "If you hadn't interfered this wouldn't be necessary," he whispered. "Want to know why, do you? You're going to die anyway so I suppose it won't hurt to satisfy your curiosity. Then you can die happy, eh?" He was holding her and preventing her from escaping, but nevertheless she managed to kick him. He threw her down with a grunt of pain and fastened a rope around her ankles before dragging her closer to the gaping hole.

"It was you remembering seeing the stupid hat. That was your death sentence. My wife knitted it for me and it was a bit of a joke. Awful it was, the pom-pom so garish I was teased about it. Your memory of seeing it near Rosie's grave might not have been enough, but I couldn't take a chance. I was there, I saw Matthew run away and went in to see what he'd been doing. I knew I hadn't time to remove the body, although

210

I knew who it was. I moved the tools after you and Glyn Howe had gone, to confuse things, muddy the waters a bit. I wasn't too worried at the discovery of her body. After all, I hadn't buried her."

Lydia pleaded with her eyes as he shone the torch at her to see the effect of his words. She would promise never to say a word if only he'd give her back her life. If only he would take off the gag and listen to her.

"Rosie was a prostitute," he went on in an almost conversational tone. "She threatened to tell everyone that the child she expected was mine. I found out later that she'd tried the same story on others – including your father. But at the time I was convinced I was the only one. She was rubbish. Not worth wrecking my career for. When I saw your father arguing with her, I finished off what she had started. Yes, she did try to kill herself, but she wasn't making a very good job of it, stabbing at her wrists ineffectually. I helped her that's all. You can hardly call it murder, can you, when I helped her commit suicide?"

Lydia tried to say, "Please," but all that came out was a low moan. He kicked her and told her to be silent. From the expression on his face, seen in the light of the torch and the brightness reflected from the pure, unsullied snow surrounding the dark scar of the grave – her grave – she could see he was enjoying the telling.

She was shivering with cold and fear. There was satisfaction on his face but, she thought with mounting terror, no mercy.

"It was pure good fortune being given the investigation. It made everything so easy. I'll show them a knife, any rusty old knife, there's plenty I can pick up in the allotment sheds. I'll say it was the one you found, a rubbishy thing and clearly nothing to do with the death of Rosie. They'll believe me." His tone had changed again, He seemed to be thinking aloud.

She began to kick, to scrape the ground with her heels, determined to leave some mark but he only laughed.

"I'm going to forget to lock the gates when I leave. Already Neville Nolan and his little band of ruffians are planning to do some sledging here tomorrow. I gave them a hint that I'd look the other way if they want to come into the castle and have some fun. Any signs of us being here will be obliterated. Good idea, eh? Snowball fights, dancing on your grave, now there's a thought, eh? Kids are entitled to some fun."

She tried again to plead but very little sound came out.

"This snow will leave the ground soggy for a while, then the frosts will harden it and by the spring there won't be a sign of you."

He lifted her by the shoulders and dragged her a few feet towards the hole in which he intended to bury her. Then he stopped and swore. Someone was approaching. Lydia tried to struggle, to kick him, tried to call out until her throat threatened to burst. But she was too securely tied.

Then there were torches. Inside the castle. Their beams swinging here and there, gradually getting nearer. Disappearing as the holders of them looked into the rooms and passageways. So close, so certain to see them.

Then the lights snapped off and she began to sob. They had given up. Tears glistened and made even the faintly glowing night sky disappear from her sight so she was surrounded by dazzling darkness.

Then, a roar of rage and two figures hurled themselves at her captor and the gag was removed, and hands were untying her feet, and Glyn's hands were chafing hers, holding her tight. He was murmuring soothing words, telling her he loved her, and she cried like a child.

The gates clanked as they were opened, and powerful lights revealed the scene. A furious Richards was held in a grip by Matthew whose tight-lipped face was a mask of fury. He had no need to hold the man so tight, he had knocked him out with one blow but he couldn't let go, needed to feel him there, in his grasp: until one of the others took him gently, assuring him that, "It's all right now sir, we have him secure. He won't get away," and Matthew gradually released his hold on the man who had killed his sister.

It was to Stella's house they went, once more the wool shop acting as the first aid post for incidents at the castle. It was there, being plied with cups of tea and endless biscuits that the full stories were told.

After she had been seen by a doctor, the police gave Lydia a lift home with Matthew and Glyn, who insisted on seeing her safely in.

Sensing that he was not needed, noticing the way Glyn fussed and Lydia enjoyed it, Matthew left, promising to call the following morning. He knew he wouldn't. Lydia was not for him. The way she and Glyn looked at each other told him that. He went back to the hotel to pack his bag. Tomorrow, once he had notified the police of his intentions, he would return to pick up his other life and plan a future without Lydia. For a while he had hoped. But whoever said, "you can never go back," was right – at least in this instance. It would have been better for everyone if he had stayed away.

"Shouldn't you be getting home too?" Lydia said to Glyn, stifling a yawn. "Won't Cath be waiting for you?" Her mind rang with the echoes of his words when he found her only a few short hours before. He had said he loved her, but now, back down to earth, she knew that was the joy of the moment, of finding her in time, with the realisation in the forefront of his mind of what would have happened if he'd arrived even a few minutes later.

"Cath, *my* Cath, is always in bed at seven," he said then, looking at her strangely.

"At seven? Is she ill?"

"Little girls need to get to sleep early. She has a hot drink, then it's teeth cleaned and a story, before settling down to sleep."

"Oh, you're talking about little Cath, I meant your Cath, her aunt."

"Little Cath *is* my Cath. Her father was a close friend of mine, and when Cath's mother died, he had to leave the Navy to make a home for her. They only had a couple of small, rented rooms. The three of us who served with him; Trevor Beacon, Danny Tremain and I decided that, as there was no insurance, no house or anything, we would give him twenty-five thousand pounds to get a business going. It isn't much, but it will enable him to borrow enough to buy a house of sorts and start a garden maintenance business. He's a genius with engines. Again, it won't be much, but it will be enough to keep them together."

"I don't understand," she said, hope beginning to grow. "Then you and Cath aren't – you and she don't . . .?"

"We all agreed that if we were going to do something like this we had to make sure we weren't doing it for the glory. We don't want anyone to know. Doing it so people would admire us would have been wrong. Everything would have been tainted and spoilt.

"We did it because we wanted to help a little girl who might otherwise have a very lonely and unhappy life. We are her uncles. Uncle Danny and Uncle Trev and me – Uncle Glyn. So far she has ten thousand from me – no, that savings account isn't mine, it belongs to Cath. The others have savings unofficially in her name too. We aren't attempting to give the same amount, just giving what we can to reach our target as swiftly as possible. A few more months and we'll have done it."

"You should have told me."

"I'd hoped that once we'd saved enough, you and I might start again without my having to explain. You're the reason I've been so desperately grabbing any opportunity to earn money. I was so afraid of losing you. But with Matthew arriving on the scene that became a forlorn hope. I knew it was too late."

"You should have trusted me, Glyn."

"I know that now. But when I thought I might, Matthew came into your life and it seemed that it didn't matter anyway."

"For a while I thought I might learn to love Matthew, but it never really happened. Poor Matthew, I treated him badly. I pretended to feel more than I did, to cover my hurt. Glyn, you should have told me."

He shook his head. "I shouldn't be telling you now, it's just that I couldn't go on with the pretence that I don't love you." He held her close and felt her shivering.

"I'll never forget that man tying me up and threatening to bury me in that hole," she whispered.

"It's all right, love. It's all right. Let's pretend it

215

was only a nightmare. I'll be near you every moment I can, to make sure you don't suffer another unhappy moment for as long as you live."

"So far as little Cath is concerned, your secret is safe," she promised. "I hope one day, when the other 'uncles' have learned to trust me, little Cath will accept me as her friend, too. A girl needs a few aunties as well as a Dad and three uncles, doesn't she? But no one will know how you and the others helped her." She touched his lips with hers to seal the promise. "It's sufficient for me to know you haven't found someone you love more," she said with a contented sigh.